"You're thinking they planted cameras so they could watch."

"Oh, my God." Both hands went to her face. "There's no other explanation."

Sean reached over and took her hand in his. "You're okay. One killer is dead, and we're onto another suspect. Whatever one or both did, it won't happen again."

She scrubbed at her eyes. "We have to search my house. Now. I need to know if they were watching me... I need to be sure."

"I think it's safe to have a look. But I'm not letting you stay there again until this is over." Sean gave her hand a squeeze before letting go.

She held his gaze. "Okay."

His entire being was aching to lean across the seat and kiss her. What he really wanted to do was pull over and make her feel this raging desire building inside him. She needed kissing. She needed to feel safe and cared for. For the first time in a very long time, he hoped he got the opportunity to make her feel that way.

STILL WATERS

USA TODAY Bestselling Author
DEBRA WEBB

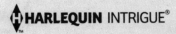
HARLEQUIN INTRIGUE®

I feel so blessed to be surrounded by wonderful,
supportive friends. Among those many amazing friends
are the members of my incredible Street Team. Thank you
for all you do and for simply being you.

ISBN-13: 978-0-373-74986-7

Still Waters

Copyright © 2016 by Debra Webb

Recycling programs
for this product may
not exist in your area.

Printed in U.S.A.

www.Harlequin.com

Debra Webb is the award-winning *USA TODAY* bestselling author of more than one hundred novels, including reader-favorite series Faces of Evil, the Colby Agency and Shades of Death. With more than four million books sold in numerous languages and countries, Debra's love of storytelling goes back to childhood on a farm in Alabama. Visit Debra at www.debrawebb.com.

Visit the Author Profile page at Harlequin.com for more titles.

CAST OF CHARACTERS

Amber Roberts—An investigative journalist, Amber is a household name in Birmingham. Now someone is determined to make the world believe she's a murderer.

Sean Douglas—Former bodyguard to Hollywood celebrities, Sean is the best at personal security. Will his own painful past cause him to fall down on the job of protecting Amber?

Jess Harris Burnett—Former FBI profiler and deputy chief of major crimes. Jess has joined forces with her old friend Buddy Corlew in a private investigations agency in an effort to help victims of crimes the police can't always resolve.

Buddy Corlew—Jess's partner and oldest friend. Buddy is a top-notch PI, but will his skills be enough?

Captain Vanessa Aldridge—The new head of crimes against persons, Aldridge dislikes reporters in general. She appears determined to make an example of Amber.

Kyle Adler—Who wanted the reclusive deliveryman dead? Was he murdered for the sole purpose of framing Amber?

Peter Thrasher—Is the mild-mannered floral shop owner arranging more than flowers?

Gerard Stevens—As an investigative reporter himself, Stevens is determined to stay on top. He fooled Amber once; has he taken his ruthlessness to the next level?

Martha Guynes—Is the kindly shop owner hiding secrets of her own?

Lori Wells, Chet Harper, Chad Cook—Detectives from Jess's former major crimes team who give her a hand whenever the need arises.

Chapter One

Fourth Avenue North
Birmingham, Alabama
Monday, October 17, 9:30 a.m.

Jess Harris Burnett had just poured her third cup of decaf when the jingle of the bell over the door sounded. As she walked toward the lobby, she heard receptionist Rebecca Scott welcoming the visitor to B&C Investigations. The office had been open almost a whole month now. Jess and her lifelong friend Buddy Corlew had made a good decision going into business together. With a nineteen-month-old daughter and a son due in a mere six weeks— Jess rubbed her enormous belly—stepping away from her position as deputy chief of Birmingham's major crimes team had been the right move.

The memory of being held prisoner by Ted Holmes attempted to bully into her thoughts, and Jess pushed it away. Holmes, like the many serial killers before him she had helped track down, was history now. Still, Jess was well aware that there would always be a new face of evil just around the next corner. She intended to leave tracking down the killers to the Birmingham PD. Her goal now was to concentrate on the victims. With B&C Investigations, she was accomplishing that goal.

"I'll let Mrs. Burnett know you're here, Ms. Coleman," Rebecca said as Jess came into the lobby.

"Gina, what brings you here this morning?" Jess flashed a smile for the receptionist. "Thank you, Rebecca. We'll be in my office."

Gina Coleman, Birmingham's beloved and award-winning television journalist, gave Jess a hug. "You look great!"

"You're the one who looks great," Jess countered. "Married life agrees with you."

Gina smiled and gave Jess another quick hug. On the way to her office, Jess grabbed her coffee and offered her friend a cup.

"No, thanks. I've had way too much already this morning."

When they were settled in Jess's office, Gina

surveyed the small space. "You've done a wonderful job of making this place comfortable."

Jess was proud of how their offices had turned out. The downtown location was good for business even if the building was a very old one. In Jess's opinion, the exposed brick walls gave the place character. It was a good fit. Anyone who knew them would say that she and Buddy had more than a little character.

"Thanks." Jess sipped her decaf and smiled. "You really do seem happy." Gina looked amazing, as always. Her long brunette hair and runway-model looks had ensured her a position in the world of television news, but it was her incredible ability to find the story that had made her a highly sought-after journalist. Her personal bravery, too, inspired Jess. Gina had taken some fire when she'd announced she was gay and married the woman she loved. Standing firm, Gina had weathered the storm.

"I am very happy." Gina stared at her hands a moment. When she met Jess's gaze once more, her face was cluttered with worry. "Barb and I need your help."

"What can I do? Name it." Jess set her coffee aside.

"A couple of hours ago Barb's younger sister, Amber, was called into the BPD about a murder."

A frown lined Jess's brow, reminding her that by the time this baby was in high school she would look like his grandmother rather than his mother. She spotted a new wrinkle every time she looked in the mirror. *Don't even go there.*

"I hadn't heard. There was a homicide last night?" This time a few months ago and Jess would have known the persons of interest and the prime suspects in every homicide long before an arrest was made in the city of Birmingham. Not anymore. Dan made it a point not to discuss work when he came home. Though she could still nudge him for details when the need arose, it was one of the perks of being married to the chief of police. A sense of well-being warmed her when she thought of her husband. He was a genuinely good man.

"Dan explained as much as he was at liberty to share. He assured me it was routine questioning, but I'm worried. I told him I was coming to you." Gina sighed. "I don't think he was very happy about my decision. He obviously prefers to keep murder and mayhem away from the mother of his children."

Two years ago Jess would have been jealous at hearing Gina had spoken to Dan. The two had once been an on-again, off-again item.

Now she counted Gina as a good friend. "Don't worry about Dan." Jess shook her head. "I've warned him time and again that just because I'm no longer a cop doesn't mean I won't be investigating murders."

"If he had his way, you'd retire," Gina teased. "We both know how he feels about keeping you safe."

Jess had been cursed with more than her fair share of obsessed killers during her career first as an FBI profiler and then as a deputy chief in the Birmingham PD. Dan's concern was understandable if unwarranted. Just because she was a mother now didn't mean she couldn't take care of herself. Admittedly, she had grown considerably more cautious.

"Tell me about the case." Considering it was a murder case, she could get the details from Lieutenant Chet Harper or Sergeant Lori Wells. Chet had recently been named acting chief of the small major crimes team—SPU, Special Problems Unit—Jess had started. Lori was reassigned to Crimes Against Persons. One or the other would be investigating the homicide case. Jess hoped the case was with Harper. She counted Lori as her best friend, but the new chief of the Crimes Against Persons Division, Captain Vanessa Aldridge, was brash and obstinate, and carried the biggest chip on her shoulder Jess had ever encountered.

Though they'd only met once or twice, Jess was familiar with Barbara's younger sister. Amber Roberts was a reporter at the same station, Channel Six, as Gina. She was young, beautiful and talented. Her and Barbara's parents were from old money, but Gina would be the first to attest to the fact that a sparkling pedigree didn't exempt one from murder. Gina's own sister had paid the price for her part in a long-ago tragedy.

"Kyle Adler's body was found in his home yesterday. He'd been stabbed repeatedly. Amber hardly knew the man. The very notion is ludicrous." Gina held up a hand. "I know you're probably thinking that I felt the same way about Julie, but this is different. Amber had nothing to do with this man's murder."

As much as Jess sympathized with Gina, Amber would not have been questioned if the police hadn't found some sort of connection between her and the victim. "The police have something," she reminded her friend. "You know this. What about the murder weapon—was it found?"

"They haven't found the murder weapon." Gina shook her head. "The whole thing is insane. Amber swears the only time she ever saw this guy was when he made a delivery to her or someone at the station. Apparently he made a living delivering for various shops around town. But the cops claim they found evidence indicating she'd been in his house. Unless someone is framing her, it simply isn't possible."

Jess chewed her bottom lip a moment. "It's conceivable someone may have wanted Adler dead and set it up to look as though another person, like Amber, committed the act."

"If that's true—" Gina leaned forward "—not only do we need help finding the actual murderer that the police may not even try to find, we also need to protect Amber. She could be in danger from the real killer."

Jess sent a text to Harper. "Let's see who's working the case first. Then we'll know whether or not we have to worry about finding the truth. As for the other, I agree. If Amber is being framed, it's quite possible she could be in danger. Personal security would be a wise step until we know what we're dealing with."

"Buddy said you do protective services as well as private investigations."

"We do," Jess agreed. "Right now the only investigator we have available is Sean Douglas."

Gina's gaze narrowed. "I'm sensing some hesitation. Do you have reservations as to whether he can handle the job?"

Jess considered how to answer the question. "He spent the past five years as a bodyguard to various celebrities in Hollywood." She shrugged. "Based on our research into his background, he was very, very good at his job. For two years prior to that he was a cop with the LAPD. He's had all the right training, and his references are impeccable."

Gina said, "There's a *but* coming."

"His last assignment was Lacy James."

Gina sat back in her chair. "Damn."

Lacy James had been a rising pop star. The rumors about drug abuse had followed her from singing in the church choir in her hometown of Memphis all the way to her Grammy nomination in LA last year.

"Her agent hired Douglas to keep an eye on her," Jess explained. "According to Douglas, she had been straight for a while and her agent wanted to ensure she stayed that way. Six months into the assignment, she died of an overdose."

Gina pressed her hands to her face, then took a breath. "Do you think what happened was in some way his fault?"

Jess shook her head. "Responsibility for what happened to Lacy James lies with her agent and her other handlers. They cared more about her career than they did her health and welfare. My only hesitation is that Douglas is a little too cocky for his own good. I think he uses attitude to cover the pain and guilt he feels about James's death." Jess paused to weigh her words. "I'm concerned his need to prove himself again might be an issue, but as for his ability to protect a client, he's more than capable."

Gina's expression brightened. "Trust me— whatever this guy's attitude, Amber can handle it. You don't rise as rapidly in my business as she has without a tough skin and a little attitude. I'm desperate, Jess. I promised Barb I would take care of this."

Jess felt confident Gina was right about Amber. Putting herself in front of the camera every day was hard work, and it wasn't for the faint of heart. "Why don't I learn all I can from the BPD and then I'll brief Douglas. I'll arrange a meeting with Amber, and we'll go from there."

"I will be forever in your debt."

"We'll take care of Amber," Jess assured her friend.

Gina stood. Jess did the same, albeit a little less gracefully.

"I'm aware that we don't always know a person as well as we believe—even the people closest to us," Gina confessed. "But I would wager all I own that Amber had nothing to do with this man's death."

Jess nodded resolutely. "Then all we need to do is ensure she stays safe until the BPD can find the killer."

Chapter Two

Forest Brook Drive, Homewood, 12:32 p.m.

Amber Roberts entered the necessary code to stop the infernal beeping of her security system, tossed her keys on the table by the door and then kicked off her heels. This had been the longest morning of her life. She closed her eyes and reminded herself to breathe as the man assigned to keep an eye on her rushed past her to have a look before she went any farther into the house.

Forcing her mind and body to focus on her normal routine, she locked the front door and set the alarm. Without waiting to hear the all-clear signal, she grabbed her shoes and headed for her bedroom. This was her home. The alarm had still been set, for God's sake. If anyone was in her house, he or she had been there since Amber left that morning. Otherwise the alarm would have gone off, right? She closed her eyes for a moment. At this point she wasn't sure of anything.

Her stomach knotted at the memory of the police showing up just as her early morning news broadcast ended. Everyone had watched as the detective explained she was needed downtown and then escorted her from the station. She didn't have to look to know her face would be plastered all over the evening papers as well as the internet and television broadcasts.

The damage control had to start now. She'd already tweeted and posted on Instagram and Facebook. The station had backed her up, as well. If the reaction didn't make her sound petty and paranoid, she would swear Gerard Stevens from the station's primary competitor had set her up.

Amber walked into her closet and shoved her shoes into their slots. Her head spun as she dragged off the dress that would forever remind her of the interview room where she'd endured a relentless interrogation by one of the BPD's finest. She tossed the dress into the dry-cleaning hamper and reached for a pair of sweatpants and a tee. Worst of all, a man was dead. Though she only knew him in passing, she felt bad about his murder. He was someone's son. Probably someone's brother and significant other. She pulled on the sweatpants. Most people had a life—unlike her. Gina and Barb warned her repeatedly that she was going to be sorry for allowing her life to fly by while she was totally absorbed by work.

Who had time for a social life? Gina should know better than anyone. Amber was fairly confident her mentor was saying what Barb expected her to say. It didn't matter either way. Amber was twenty-eight; her top priority was her career. She still had decades for falling in love and building a family.

Even if her narrow focus on her career did get lonely sometimes.

She yanked on the tee and kicked the thought aside. The police believed she was somehow involved in a man's murder. Her love life, or lack thereof, was the least of her worries.

How the hell the police could think she was involved was the million-dollar question. Why in the world would she hurt this man, much less kill him? She scarcely knew him. He had made a few deliveries to her house. He was always pleasant, but they never exchanged more than a dozen words. None of what she'd been told by the police so far made the slightest bit of sense.

"The house is clear."

Amber jumped, slamming her elbow into the wall. Frowning at the broad-shouldered man filling the doorway to her closet, she rubbed her funny bone.

"Thank you," she said even though she didn't quite feel thankful. She did not want a babysitter. She hadn't killed anyone, and there was no reason for a soul to want to harm her. Reporting the news for the past six-plus years had given her certain insights into situations like this one, and hiring a bodyguard this early in the investigation was overreacting. There could only be two potential explanations for her current dilemma: mistaken identity or a frame job. Both happened. As hard as she tried, she could come up with no other explanation.

Her bodyguard's gaze roamed from her face all the way to her toes and back with a couple of unnecessary pauses in between. Now that annoyed her. He was here to keep her safe—supposedly. He had no business looking at her as if she was the next conquest on his radar. Though she suspected Mr. Sexy-as-Hell usually didn't have to work very hard to get what he wanted. The man was gorgeous. Tall, with those broad shoulders that narrowed into a lean waist. Thick blond hair just the right length for threading your fingers through and deep blue eyes. His muscular build attested to his dedicated workout ethics. With every extra thump of her pulse she understood that beneath his smooth, tanned skin was an ego large enough for the Vulcan iron man that watched over the city of Birmingham from high atop Red Mountain.

Sean Douglas was hot, and he damn well knew it.

As if he agreed wholeheartedly with her assessment, he gifted her with a nod and disappeared.

Amber sighed. She should pull herself together. Her attorney was on the way over with whatever details the police had shared with him. They'd done nothing but ask questions this morning. Each time her attorney had asked about the evidence, the detective had evaded the question. Still, she hadn't needed a lawyer to tell her that she wouldn't have been called in and so thoroughly questioned had there been no evidence. Friends, colleagues and people acquainted with the victim were questioned in their homes or workplaces. Only the ones about to be named a person of interest—or, worse, a suspect—were hauled to the station and interviewed. The police had wanted her off balance—which was not a good thing.

How the hell was this possible?

She needed a couple of cocktails and a good night's sleep. Maybe she'd wake up in the morning and discover this had all been just one big old bad nightmare.

Finding Sean Douglas kicked back on the sofa in her living room reminded her that the situation was all too real.

"I put on a pot of coffee." He leaned forward and braced his forearms on his knees. "I figured some caffeine would be useful the next few hours."

She would have preferred a caramel latte, but she'd been too emotional to think of dropping by her favorite coffee shop after leaving the police department. Her parents were beside themselves. They were in a remote part of Africa on a medical aid mission and couldn't get back for days. She and Barbara had insisted they stay and do the important work they'd gone there to do. This entire business was nothing more than a mistake. Surely it would be cleared up in a day or two.

Belatedly she remembered to say, "Thank

you." Her attorney, Frank Teller, was a coffee drinker. Vaguely she wondered how Douglas had known this or if he was a coffee guy, too.

"I can call in some lunch for delivery. I'm guessing you didn't take time for breakfast this morning."

She appreciated the offer but said, "I had a protein smoothie. I'm fine."

He dismissed her response with a wave of his hand. "How about a pizza or a burger? Your choice."

She couldn't possibly eat. "I'm not hungry. Feel free to raid my kitchen or order something for yourself."

His mouth eased into a lopsided grin. "Already done that. You're fresh out of real food."

A frown furrowed her brow. He'd prowled through her kitchen? What kind of bodyguard checked the fridge?

"Why don't you tell me about yourself," he suggested with a pat of the sofa cushion next to him.

Amber felt sure that inviting pat worked well for him under normal circumstances, but those blue eyes and that hopeful smile did little more than annoy her at the moment. "Weren't you briefed on my case?"

The need for personal security was entirely

new to her, but instinct told her a man assigned to protect her would certainly have been briefed about the situation. Small talk was the furthest thing from her mind. He needed to find a way to entertain himself if he was bored. She had no desire to chat.

"I was." He clasped his hands between his spread thighs.

"What else do you need to know?" She gave herself a mental pat on the back for not sounding as snippy as she felt.

"Until this situation is resolved," he began, tracking her movements with those blue eyes as she settled in a chair a few feet away, "we'll be spending a lot of time together. It's helpful to know a little more than the facts of the case. What time do you like to get up in the mornings? What's your usual bedtime? Do you watch television or read or just relax in the evenings? Should I expect company? Is there a boyfriend to accommodate?" He shrugged. "Things like that are good to know."

For the love of Mike. Amber shook off the frustration. His request had merit. *No need to be unreasonable.* "I'm up at six unless I'm called to a scene earlier or I host the morning news the way I did this morning. I go to bed right after the ten o'clock news assuming

I haven't been called out to a scene. I usually leave the television turned on all night." She glanced at the dark screen hanging on the wall above her fireplace. She imagined that every channel was running stories about her and the murder. "I might be taking a break from that habit for a few days."

"Understandable." He cocked an eyebrow. "What about a boyfriend?"

"There is no boyfriend." Somehow saying it out loud sounded far worse than simply knowing it. She hadn't been in a serious relationship in more than a year. Maybe there wouldn't be another one. Who had time? More important, who cared? She had everything she needed. *If that's so, why the sudden need to justify your status?*

He made a knowing sound as something like surprise flashed across his face. "A girlfriend then?"

"No girlfriend."

He made one of those male grunts that could convey surprise as easily as indifference. Either way, the sound got on her already-frazzled nerves.

"Your degree is in mass communications," he said, changing the subject. "When did you decide you preferred working in front of the camera versus behind it?"

"I didn't decide. The journalist I assisted during my first assignment was in a car accident. Everyone was on the scene except her and the cameraman told me to get in front of the camera and do the job. The audience responded well to me, so that's where the powers that be decided I should be—on-screen."

"But you had aspirations?"

Amber nodded. "I had my heart set on hosting one of the big entertainment news shows." She laughed, remembering the horror on her parents' faces when she'd told them. "It wasn't exactly the career my family had hoped for."

He smiled. It was nice. Really nice. *Too nice, damn it.* "Your parents and your sister are all doctors."

"Yes. I'm the black sheep." The realization that her words had never been truer stole the air from her lungs. Now she was a potential suspect in a homicide.

The doorbell saved her from going down that pity path. She stood to go to the door, but Douglas moved ahead of her and checked the security viewfinder.

"It's Mr. Teller."

Douglas opened the door, and Teller came

inside. He'd already been introduced to the man who would be keeping watch over her. There was just something wrong with calling him a bodyguard. Particularly since she continued to have a bit of trouble keeping her attention off *his* body. The foolish reaction had to be about sex. She hadn't been intimate with anyone since she and Josh had ended their relationship.

Her gaze drifted to the man assigned to protect her. *Don't even go there.*

"We should speak privately," Frank Teller announced before saying hello. He looked from Amber to Douglas and back.

"I'd like him to stay," Amber countered. Douglas and his boss would need to be kept up to speed anyway.

When Teller relented, Douglas insisted on serving the coffee. Amber was happy to let him do the honors. Her knees were feeling a little weak as she sank back into a chair. Maybe it was the grim expression Teller wore.

He placed his briefcase on the coffee table and opened it. "The news is not good."

Amber's stomach did the sinking now. "What sort of evidence could they possibly have? I don't even know this man! He…he made deliveries to my house and the station a couple of times." Maybe more than a couple of times. Still, the whole thing was incredible.

"Amber." Teller closed his briefcase and placed the folder he'd removed atop it. "I've known your family for most of my life. Your father is my father's personal physician. Your mother was my pediatrician. I, of all people, know this is wrong. You couldn't possibly have harmed this man. Yet the evidence is enough to make even me have second thoughts."

The trembling she had experienced that morning after the initial shock that no one was playing a joke on her started anew. The police had mentioned evidence without providing the details. "What evidence? I don't know how they could find evidence that leads back to me in a home where I've never been…on a body I've never touched."

"They found a teacup with your prints on it."

"What?" The situation had just gone from unbelievable to incomprehensible. "If there is anything in that poor man's house that either belonged to me or bore my prints, someone— besides me—put it there."

Before Teller could respond, Douglas returned with the coffee. He'd gone to the trouble to find her grandmother's serving tray and to dig out the china cups and saucers rather than the stoneware mugs. He'd even prepared the creamer and sugar servers. Her disbelief was temporarily sidelined by the idea that he would think to go to so much trouble.

Douglas placed the tray on the coffee table, and she noted there were only two cups. "If you need me for anything—" he hitched his thumb toward the rear of the house "—I'll be outside checking the perimeter."

"Thank you." Amber suddenly didn't want anyone else to hear these incredible lies—at least not until she had heard them.

When Douglas was gone, Teller said, "Amber, I realize this is shocking."

He'd certainly nailed her feelings with that statement. "I don't understand how any of this happened." She shook her head, overwhelmed and confused and, honestly, terrified. "You see it on television or in the movies, but this is real life. *My* life."

"Do you drink a tea called Paradise Peach?"

Something cold and dark welled inside her. She moistened her lips and cleared her throat. "Yes. It's my favorite. There's a specialty shop downtown that stocks it."

"A can of Paradise Peach tea was found in the victim's home. Your prints were on the can."

Worry furrowed her brow and bumped

her pulse rate to a faster rhythm. "Maybe he shopped there, too. He may have picked up a can after I did." Hope knotted in her chest, but it was short-lived. How did a person prove a theory as full of circumstantial holes as the one she'd just suggested?

"Certainly," he agreed. "Bear in mind that the burden of proof is not ours. It will be up to the BPD to make their case. For that they need evidence, which brings us to the cup that also bore your prints."

The rationale she had attempted to use earlier vanished. Dear Lord she felt as if she had just awakened in the middle of a horror film and she was the next victim. All she had to do now was scream.

"Take a look at these crime scene photos." He opened the folder and removed two eight-by-ten photographs. He scooted his briefcase and the serving platter to the far side of the table and placed the photographs in front of her. "These are copies, so they're not the best quality."

The first one showed the victim lying on the floor next to the dining table in what she presumed was his kitchen. Blood had soaked his shirt. He appeared to have multiple stab wounds to the chest. *Poor man.* She swallowed back the lump of emotion that rose in her throat and moved on to the second one. The second was a wider-angle view showing more of the room. Definitely the kitchen. Her attention zeroed in on the table. The table was set for two. Teacups sat in matching saucers, each flanked by a spoon and linen napkin. She squinted at the pattern on the cups. A floral pattern for sure, but difficult to distinguish.

"He was having tea with someone." She lifted her gaze to Teller's. "Whoever that person was, he or she is likely the one who killed him. Based on the prints found at the scene, the police believe that person was you."

Hands shaking, she pressed her fingers to her mouth to hold back the cry of outrage. "The medical examiner is certain about the time of death?"

Teller nodded. "Last Friday night, around eight. It'll be a while before we have the autopsy results, which will tell us what he had for dinner and various other details that may or may not help our case."

Amber made a face.

"Knowing what and where he ate might help us," Teller explained. "The police might be able to track down the restaurant—if he ate out—and someone there might remember if he was alone."

Sounded like a long shot to her. The detectives had pressed her over and over about her whereabouts on Friday night. It was the one time she'd come home early and hit the sack. She hadn't spent any time doing research at the station, she hadn't spoken to anyone and she'd had no company. None of her neighbors could confirm she was home. She hadn't done any work on her home computer, which might have confirmed her whereabouts. Bottom line, she had no alibi.

Disgusted, she shook her head. "Single people all over the world should be terrified of spending a quiet evening at home alone." If she were married or involved in a relationship, she might have spent time or at least spoken to her plus one that evening.

"There's more."

His somber tone caused her heart to skip a beat.

"A pair of panties were found in his bed. There was trace evidence. A pubic hair and a much longer hair…" He touched his head. "They want you to agree to a DNA test."

The heart that had stumbled a moment ago slammed against her ribs now. "Do you think

I should?" Considering her fingerprints were there, she couldn't help but feel somewhat tentative as to how to proceed. "I know I haven't been in his house or his bed, so I have nothing to hide, but my fingerprints were there." She pressed a hand to her throat. "If someone is setting me up…"

He reached into his folder and removed another photograph. "Do you recognize these?"

The red panties in the photograph stole her ability to draw in air. She shot to her feet and rushed to her bedroom. Opening drawer after drawer, she rifled through her things and then slammed each door closed in turn. Her pulse pounding, she moved to the laundry hamper.

The panties weren't there.

Teller stood at her bedroom door, worry lining his face. "Lots of women have red panties. My wife has red panties. How can you be sure you recognize these?"

Her lungs finally filled with air. "The little bows." She paused to release the big breath she'd managed to draw in. "There should be a little satin red bow on each side. One is missing. It annoys me every time I see it. I've meant to throw them away…"

Of course any woman with red panties that sported little red bows could be missing a bow. In her gut, Amber knew better than to believe it was a mere coincidence. Her red one-bowed panties were missing. There was a tea-cup in the man's house, for God's sake, with her prints on it. She didn't need a DNA test to prove a damned thing. The hair and any other trace evidence would be hers, as well. Whoever wanted her to appear guilty had done a bang-up job.

Douglas appeared behind Teller. "Is everything okay?"

No. Everything was not okay. In fact, nothing was okay.

"I'll do the DNA test," Amber said to the man representing her.

Teller gave her a resigned nod. "I'll set it up."

Dear God. She was in serious trouble here.

Chapter Three

The mouthpiece hung around awhile longer, asking more questions and making Amber even more upset. Sean had heard of the guy. All the rich folks in Jefferson County used him. Teller didn't need billboards or commercials with catchy jingles. The family name got him all the business he would ever need. It didn't hurt that he had a reputation for being the best damn attorney in town.

Sean turned his attention back to assessing Amber's place. If the items found in the victim's residence were Amber's and she hadn't put them there, someone had been in her home. The reality likely hadn't sunk in for her just yet. It would hit her soon enough. It was time to start considering who would want to see Amber go down for murder. There had to be an old schoolmate or ex-bestie, maybe even a competitor at a rival television station with a grudge against her. Revenge, jealousy, there were all kinds of potential motives.

No matter that he'd only been employed at B&C Investigations for a month, he'd learned a lot from the boss already. Jess had a motto: find the motive, find the killer. When looking for the source of trouble, there was no better advice. The boss didn't exactly have a lot of confidence in Sean just yet. She'd been reluctant to assign him this case—which was exactly why he had to do the best job possible. Of course, he always wanted to do a good job, but he couldn't allow even a single misstep this time. He had a feeling the first mistake and he would be out at B&C Investigations.

For damned sure he would never again allow the kind of mistake he'd made on his last security assignment. His bad judgment had cost a life.

His fingers stilled on the back door's lock mechanism. How could he blame Jess Burnett for not fully trusting him? No matter that he had years of outstanding work history under his belt, his last assignment for his former employer had gone to hell. The only reason he'd gotten the job with B&C Investigations was because Buddy Corlew and Sean's older brother, Chase, were friends. They'd played high school football together—against each other, actually. Chase had warned Sean that a year of moping around was enough. Sean had to get on with his life. During his time in Hollywood he'd built up considerable savings. Private security in the entertainment world paid extremely well. Finding a new job hadn't been necessary the first year after he returned home, but his brother was right. Sean had to get on with at least part of his life. His personal life might never recover from his mistake with Lacy, but there was no excuse for allowing his professional life to stay in the toilet.

"Is there something wrong with my door?"

Amber's question snapped him from his worrisome thoughts. He closed the door and shook his head. "I've checked front and back doors, and so far no sign of forced entry. The windows are next."

A frown dragged down the corners of her lips. She had nice lips. Full and pink. Her red hair and green eyes were a vivid contrast to her pale skin. The sprinkling of freckles across her nose she worked so hard to cover with makeup made him want to smile. She was a gorgeous lady, no doubt, but not the kind of overdone Hollywood beauty he'd disliked in California.

Amber's was natural and completely unpretentious. He'd been watching her and fantasizing for months.

Fantasies and casual encounters were all he had anymore. He wasn't sure he would ever trust himself in a real relationship again, and he would never permit work to become personal. Of course, his brother warned him that a guy still six months from thirty shouldn't be throwing in the towel.

Realization dawned in the lady's pretty green eyes. "You think someone broke into my home and took my...the evidence the police found." The frown reappeared. "But how did they get my prints on the teacup?"

When he looked confused, she quickly explained about the evidence the BPD had discovered in the murder victim's home.

Sean inspected the second of three kitchen windows. "Trust me," he said in answer to her question, "there are ways to get into any place—home or business—if a person wants in badly enough."

Amber followed him into the living room. She watched silently as he confirmed the windows were locked and that all the locking mechanisms were in working order.

"You mean like overriding security codes?"

"That's one way, yes." He shrugged. "Folks who make it their business to break and enter can unlock about any kind of lock with or without a key."

Rather than continue with her hovering too close and watching his every move, he decided to run a few questions by her. Why not start with the most obvious ones she'd already answered for his boss and more than likely for the police? "Do you have any enemies, Amber?"

Her arms crossed protectively over her chest, and she dropped into the nearest chair. "Your boss and the police asked me that question along with a barrage of others. The answer is no. I've never had any sort of trouble with anyone. I've never had a stalker. Never received strange emails or Facebook messages. The fan mail from viewers is never threatening or overly negative. Someone might disagree with the way I reported an issue or event, but so far no one has taken it any further."

"Lucky you. Most celebrities get their fair share of threatening or nasty mail." Sean meant the comment as a compliment, but judging by her sigh she didn't feel so lucky. He hitched his head toward the hall that led to the bedrooms. "How about persistent fans or admirers? Any of those?"

Amber pushed to her feet and trailed after him. "The usual. I typically receive flowers at the station a couple of times a week, depending on the stories I've covered. The high-profile stories generate the most reaction from viewers. Letters, food baskets, the occasional gift." She rubbed at the back of her neck and then stretched it from side to side. "Nothing negative."

The single window in the hall bath was secure. Sean moved to the first of the three bedrooms. "Any that are unsigned or from repeat senders?"

"A few."

Both windows in bedroom one were secure. "Define 'a few.'"

Following him to the next bedroom, she shrugged and said, "Four or five fans who consistently send little gifts. The occasional unsigned letter, maybe once or twice a month."

"Have you ever met any of the four or five gift senders?" He progressed from the first window to the second before moving on to the final bedroom—her private space.

"The station has a big community day twice a year." She crossed her arms over her chest, drawing his errant attention momentarily to her breasts. "You know, to thank the viewers.

We do photos and giveaways. Have games and hot dogs. There's always a clown and a couple of cartoon characters for the kids. Sometimes the people who write to me or send me gifts or flowers come by and say hi. No drama or discomfort. Just a friendly hello and a request for an autograph."

The instant he entered her bedroom he felt completely out of place. The room smelled like her. Whatever perfume she wore was restrained but unmistakable. Light and citrusy. The delicate fragrance was barely there but so uniquely her, as if the subtle sweetness came from all that soft, satiny skin. He gave his head a mental shake. Evidently the skintight tee she wore had his imagination running a little wild.

The bed was big, too large for a woman to lie in alone. The bedding was pure white, lush and natural—like Amber. It didn't take much to summon the image of that long, curly red hair flowing over those white linens. His body tightened with need at the thought of climbing onto that bed and kissing his way up her naked body.

Do the job, man. "Do you keep the unsigned letters?" He walked to the nearest window and confirmed it was locked. "Some of those may be from the same person."

She massaged her temples as if a headache had begun there. Who wouldn't have a headache? She was a person of interest in a murder case. That was enough to give anyone a headache.

"I never looked to see if there were similarities in the handwriting. I don't keep them all. Only the ones that touch me in some way. In fact, Gina and I did a special about how feedback from viewers added a richness to our work." She smiled; his pulse reacted. "We each shared things about ourselves that viewers could hopefully relate to. It was one of the most watched local programs last year."

Her bedroom windows were secure. He stepped into the en suite bath. The only window was one of the half-moon types above the shower and it didn't open. Like the rest of her home, the bathroom was organized and well-appointed. The house was a traditional one-story brick in an upscale, older neighborhood. According to the background report Jess had given him, Amber had lived here since graduating college. She'd inherited the house from her grandmother.

He returned to the bedroom, where she waited in the middle of the room looking very much like a lost little girl. "You keep the fan mail here or at work?"

"Here." She opened the double doors leading to what he presumed would be the closet.

He hesitated in the doorway. The closet was almost as large as the bedroom with a sliding library-style ladder that provided access to the upper shelves that banded all the way around the space above the hanging clothes.

"The house used to have four bedrooms," she explained as she adjusted the ladder. "I used the fourth bedroom to expand the bathroom and for this closet."

"Looks like you made a smart move." He surveyed the rods and rods of clothes and the rows of shoes and whistled. "This could be a supermodel's closet."

"Ha-ha. Viewers notice if you wear the same outfit." She climbed up the ladder and reached for a box covered in a floral pattern resting on the first shelf.

"Let me take that." He stepped over to the ladder and reached up to take the box.

"I suppose you'd know a supermodel's closet when you saw one. My sister told me you were a bodyguard to the stars."

He accepted the box and waited for her to

climb down the few rungs. "I may have seen one or two."

She pushed the ladder back into its storage position. "Don't be modest, Mr. Douglas. Barbara says you had quite the reputation in Hollywood as a top security specialist as well as a ladies' man."

Apparently she hadn't heard the whole story. "Where do you want these?" He was damned ready to get out of her bedroom. Being surrounded by her scent and her private things in what now felt like a small space was too much.

"Kitchen table."

Rather than be a gentleman and wait for her to go first, he got the hell out of her closet and her bedroom. A few deep breaths and he still hadn't cleared her scent from his lungs. He shook off the uneasiness and placed the box on the round table that stood in the breakfast alcove of the kitchen.

The red and pink rose-patterned box wasn't a typical file storage size. Handholds were formed on each end. Judging by the weight, it was made of heavy-gauge cardboard. He'd noted several of varying sizes on the uppermost shelf of her closet. Some he recognized as photograph boxes. All were neatly arranged by size and color. His mother had similar tastes and organizing habits. From what he'd seen so far, his mother would like Amber.

He booted the concept out of his head. Maybe he needed more coffee. He was sure as hell having a hard time keeping his head on straight.

Amber joined him at the table. She pressed a hand to her flat belly and made a face.

"Look." He took her by the shoulders and turned her to face him. "I know you TV personalities don't like to eat for fear of gaining half an ounce, but you're going through some serious trauma right now. You need to eat."

Her green eyes were wide with surprise or indignation because he'd touched her or that he'd dared to give her an order or both. He released her and dropped his hands back to his sides.

"No need for strong-arm tactics, Mr. Douglas. I was just thinking that I needed to eat." She turned gracefully and marched to the refrigerator.

Strong-arm tactics? Well, at least she was smart enough to listen to good advice.

She pulled open the freezer drawer and selected a frozen dinner—the organic, calorie-conscious kind. While she removed the outer packaging, she flashed him a fake smile and said, "Take your pick. I highly recommend the pecan chicken and rice."

While she nuked her meal, he rummaged through the selection. He chose the pizza. The photo on the box looked normal enough, though he doubted one would ever be enough. The way his stomach was protesting, he could eat his weight in steak and potatoes about now.

"Water or coffee?" She grabbed a bottle of water from the fridge for herself.

"Water would be great."

Ten minutes later they were seated at the table with their little prepackaged meals—*little* being the operative word. The first bite of the pizza did two things. Burned the hell out of his mouth and confirmed that although it looked nothing like the one on the box, it tasted exactly like the box.

"Gina says you grew up in Birmingham." She twirled her fork in the noodles of her meal. She'd picked out the little chicken and broccoli chunks.

He imagined the noodles tasted somewhat similar to his pizza. "I did. When I graduated high school I went for a criminal justice degree. After that I headed out to Cali with my best friend. We both went to work for the LAPD. My friend's parents had divorced when he was a kid. His father promised him a job with the department if he wanted to move out to California after school."

"So you both became cops?"

He tore off another chunk of the tasteless pizza and nodded. "Two years later the top personal security team in the LA area offered me a position with a salary I couldn't refuse."

"You must have done something to grab their attention?" She smiled, and his pulse executed another of those crazy dips.

"I might have saved a couple of lives in a nightclub shoot-out while off duty and without a firearm." He shoved the last of the pizza into his mouth to prevent having to say more. The doped-up ex-husband who'd come after his wife in a crowded club with a cocked and loaded nine millimeter had every intention of killing anyone in the room with her. There hadn't been time to think, only to act. Sean had thrown himself at the guy. Two shots had hissed by his head, close enough to have him wishing he'd gone to church a little more often. Clips from the club's security cameras had played on all the local networks and even a couple of national ones for days. The notoriety had bothered him. He'd done the right thing. Maybe that might have made him a hero to some.

"Had you always envisioned yourself as a bodyguard to the stars?" Amber set her fork aside and sipped her water.

"Never crossed my mind until they knocked on my door."

"What was it like? Are the big stars as difficult to work with as the gossip rags suggest?"

He really didn't want to talk about his past. Things always ventured into the territory he still couldn't revisit. The only reason he hadn't changed the subject already was because she looked relaxed for the first time since they'd met.

"Stars are like anyone else. You've got the nice ones, and you've got the jerks. They put on their pants the same way you and I do."

"According to Gina, you're the best."

He pushed back from the table and stood. "Your friend might have exaggerated just a little." He carried his plate to the sink and rinsed it before depositing it into the dishwasher. Amber did the same with her bowl and fork.

"We need a notepad or something to list the names of the people who've written to you repeatedly." He moved back to the table. The sooner they focused on the reason he was here, the quicker she would forget about all the questions she appeared to have for him. Not that he had expected anything less from the lady. Amber might not be a big-screen celebrity, but she was damned sure a big star in Birmingham. "Anyone who seems overly interested in your career or you as a person is what we're looking for."

She opened a drawer and came up with a notepad and pen.

"We should talk about your neighbors," he went on. "Friends. Ex-boyfriends. Former girlfriends. Anyone who knows your routine. Anyone who knows you well enough to have a handle on your likes and dislikes. Paradise Peach tea, for instance. Who would know about your taste in tea?"

When she'd settled back at the table, she placed the pen next to the pad and looked him straight in the eye. "My sister and my parents. My colleagues at work. None of them would do this any more than I would. Most of my neighbors are the same ones who lived here when my grandmother was still alive. They're older, and I've known them forever. I have no former girlfriends. I only have current ones."

"No fallings-out. No estrangements of any kind?"

"There are people with whom I've lost touch, but nothing like you're suggesting."

"What about ex-boyfriends? Even the one-night stands—especially the one-night stands."

"I don't do one-night stands, Mr. Douglas. This is not Hollywood."

"But it is the twenty-first century. Even people in Alabama do one-night stands, Ms. Roberts."

"Not this person." Her eyebrows shot up her forehead. "And before you jump to that conclusion, I'm not a prude, either."

"Ex-boyfriends?"

"We talked about this already."

He exhaled a big breath and reached for patience. "I need more details."

"There have been three."

Did she just say three? "Three?" he echoed.

She gave him a sharp look that answered the question. "One in high school. We started dating when we were freshmen. We broke up when we went our separate ways to college. He's married with three children and lives in Wyoming. My second boyfriend was in college. He decided he wanted to travel the world before settling down. To my knowledge he's still doing so. Last year I broke up with the man to whom I'd been engaged for two years."

"Please tell me you dated a few guys in between."

"A few. Yes. I was very busy with my education and then with building my career, Mr. Douglas."

"Sean," he countered. "The Mr. Douglas thing makes me feel old."

"I certainly wouldn't want to make you feel old, *Sean*," she acquiesced.

Like every other ridiculous reaction he'd experienced since coming into her home, the sound of his first name on those pink lips disrupted the rhythm of his pulse again. "The ex-fiancé has no reason to want to cause you trouble?"

She sent him a look. "Killing a man and leaving my panties in his bed is a little more than causing me trouble—wouldn't you say?"

He nodded. She had him there. "I'll take that as a no."

"We broke up because he confessed that he'd never stopped loving his college sweetheart. They're married with a baby on the way. They live in Mobile. I'm certain I'm the last person on his mind these days."

The guy must have been a total idiot.

Sean cleared his throat and his head. "That leaves us with strangers." More often than not, crimes of this nature were committed by an intimate, but not always. Occasionally strangers formed fantasy relationships or attachments with high-profile personalities. Once in a while those bonds led to murder.

"Okay." She stood, took the lid from the box and set it aside. "I have quite a few letters and cards here." She reached inside and lifted a mound of envelopes. She placed them on the table. She reached into the box once more and stalled. "What in the world?" Her eyes widened with horror. "Oh, my God."

Sean moved to her side. In the box, amid the stacks of envelopes addressed to Amber Roberts, was a knife. Nothing elaborate or exotic, just a stock kitchen butcher knife, with an eight-or ten-inch blade covered in dried blood.

It was time to call his boss.

Chapter Four

Captain Vanessa Aldridge stared directly at Amber. "You want me to believe that you just happened to have a knife from the victim's kitchen in your home. A knife, I might add, that is covered in his blood."

The head of the Crimes Against Persons Division had asked Amber this same question several different ways over the past three hours. The lab had confirmed the blood on the knife was in fact Kyle Adler's. The knife apparently was part of a set from his home. Dear God, how had this happened? Why would anyone do this to her? Her home had been searched by the forensic team for any other potential evidence. It was all completely insane.

"Your prints are on the knife handle, Ms. Roberts."

Amber blinked. Her mind wouldn't stay focused on the moment.

"Of course her prints are on the handle," Teller countered. "She touched it while she was searching through a box of saved fan mail."

"Do you have some way of proving her prints weren't already there?" Aldridge argued.

"Do you have some way of proving they were?" Teller fired back. "I have no burden to prove anything, as you well know. You're the one who needs to prove your accusations. And unless you can do that, Captain Aldridge, I would suggest you stop harassing my client."

Amber felt sick. "I have never seen that knife before. I have no idea how it got in my house."

Teller put his hand on her arm to silence her. He didn't want her to make any spontaneous remarks. Only the prepared ones they had discussed before this meeting. This was wrong. All of it. And it was escalating. She was terrified at the idea of what might happen next. It felt surreal, like someone else's life was spiraling out of control.

"You have a security system. Who else

knows the access code?" Aldridge demanded for the third time.

"My client is uncertain of the answer," Teller replied without hesitation.

"You don't recall who you gave something as important as your security code? An old boyfriend? An associate from work? You can't expect me to believe you have no idea who else might have access to your own home."

The captain stared directly at her, ensuring Amber understood the questions and comments were meant for her regardless of the attorney seated beside her. Amber merely stared back. She'd already answered those questions. Teller had reminded her repeatedly not to allow Aldridge to drag her into a discussion. The captain's job, according to Teller, was to trip Amber up and make her say something she didn't mean. The truth was, Amber couldn't have answered at the moment even if Teller had wanted her to. Some level of shock had descended, and she couldn't think quickly enough to piece together a proper response.

"Ms. Roberts, I'm aware your attorney is supposed to work in your best interest, but frankly I'm concerned as to why he feels compelled to answer for you—if you have nothing to hide."

Teller launched a protest.

Amber held up her hands. "Are we done here?" They had been at this for three hours. Her answers weren't going to change whether she gave the prepared ones or the ones straight from her heart—assuming she could get the right words out. "Or do you plan to arrest me?"

Aldridge laid one hand atop the other on the table and smiled. "We're done for now, but rest assured, Ms. Roberts, we will be speaking again. Soon, so don't leave town."

Amber wanted out of this room. She tried to slow her racing heart, tried to still her churning stomach. *Who would do this?* The question echoed in her brain. She could think of no one who wanted to hurt her this way.

Captain Aldridge walked to the door, glancing over her shoulder one last time before exiting. The silence that ensued left Amber feeling hollow and alone.

"Let's get you home."

Amber followed Teller's prompts and exited the interview room. Douglas—Sean waited in the corridor.

"We're going out the back," he said to Teller.

Teller nodded. "I'll go out the front and hopefully keep the media entertained long enough to allow the two of you to escape.

Escape. Amber had been one of those reporters more times than she could count. Desperate to get the story. Determined to discover what the person in the spotlight was hiding. Certain the police were holding back crucial information.

"No." Amber shook her head. "I'm not running from the press."

Teller urged her to listen to reason as they boarded the elevator. She ignored him. As the doors opened into the lobby, he launched a final plea. "I can't do my job if you don't cooperate. Every step you take makes an impression. If this case goes to trial, the jury will be made up of people who watch the news and read the paper."

Amber had had enough. She turned to him. "I'm certain you'll be able to do your job under whatever circumstances arise, Frank."

Teller held up his hands and backed off. "I've said my piece."

As she approached the main entrance, Sean pulled her close. "I'm not going to try to talk you out of something you're obviously intent on doing, but we will do it my way." Her gaze locked with his as he went on. "You will stay right beside me. You will not reach out to anyone who reaches toward you. You will stay focused on moving forward while giving whatever responses you intend to give quickly and concisely."

His eyes and the stony set of his jaw warned there would be no changing his mind. Unable to do otherwise, Amber nodded her agreement.

"Good. Let's do this." He pushed through the door, moving her along with confident strides.

Lights flashed and questions were hurled at her. As Sean had predicted, hands extended toward her. Amber felt as if she were being pulled in every direction. The few faces she recognized blurred with the many she did not.

"Amber, did you murder Kyle Adler?"

"Amber, have you been arrested?"

"Amber, were you and Kyle involved?"

She wanted to answer. Her feet stumbled, and her tongue felt tied. Her heart pushed into her throat.

"Give us your side, Amber!" a vaguely familiar voice shouted.

Behind her, Teller assured the crowd that Amber had not been arrested and was not involved with Kyle Adler. He firmly stated that she certainly had not murdered him.

Sean pushed his way through the microphones and the cameras stretching toward them. Amber moved along in his wake, able to remain upright and progress forward only because he held tightly to her arm.

They reached his car, and suddenly she was in the passenger seat. He slid behind the wheel, and they started to roll slowly through the seemingly endless crowd. The situation was completely alien to her. She felt lost and uncertain. This was what she did every day. How could she feel so completely out of place on this side of the story? Where was her professional training? Where was her courage? She should have answered those questions. She should have looked directly into the camera and told the world that she was innocent no matter what Sean or Teller told her to do.

How many times had she watched someone do exactly what she just did and doubted the veracity of his or her claims of innocence?

People watching the news would think precisely that about her. They would believe she'd killed a man. They would believe she knew all the tricks to avoid being found guilty because she was a reporter. They would believe she was lying because her job was to spin stories into the kind of news viewers couldn't resist.

"I'm telling the truth." She turned to Sean

as he accelerated, leaving the horde of reporters behind. "I *am* telling the truth."

He glanced at her. "I believe you."

Did anyone else?

"We're going to the office," he explained as he made the next turn. "My boss wants to speak with you."

Amber managed a nod. His boss was former deputy chief Jess Burnett. Gina trusted her. Amber had been working her way up the ranks when Jess first returned to Birmingham. She remembered the buzz about the FBI's top profiler helping with the Murray case. No one would ever forget how serial killer Eric Spears had followed Jess here. Amber had read the stories about her and how she could find the face of evil when no one else could.

Please let her be able to find this one.

Fourth Avenue North

"Amber, I know this is unsettling."

Amber produced a smile for Jess Burnett. "I never thought I'd say this, but yes, this is terrifying." Had she been such a coward all this time?

"Being the target of breaking news is far different from finding the breaking news. Trust me on that one," Jess assured her.

Certainly the former profiler would know. Amber remembered well when Jess had been the target of those who thought she'd brought evil to town with her—that she was on some level partially responsible for the heinous murders committed by Eric Spears and his followers.

"I appreciate that you understand," Amber confessed. "What I really want to hear is that you can help prove I'm telling the truth. I don't think Captain Aldridge believes me."

"We'll do all we can—you have our word on that," Buddy Corlew assured her.

Buddy sat next to Jess. Amber knew a little about him, as well. He'd grown up in a rough neighborhood and he'd beaten the odds. He'd served in the military and the Birmingham Police Department. Even when his career as a detective had tanked, he'd built a thriving private investigation agency. The man was a fighter as well as the new husband of the recently named Jefferson County medical examiner.

If the people in this room couldn't help her prove her innocence, Amber felt reasonably confident she was screwed.

Next to her Sean shifted in his chair as if

he'd read her mind and recognized that she had left him out of her deduction. Bearing in mind that they'd found a bloody knife in her house—which confirmed beyond all doubt that someone had been in her home without her knowledge—she was pretty damned sure she needed him, too. And her attorney, Frank Teller, was the best. Amber would need them all to get through this nightmare.

"We didn't invite Teller to this meeting," Corlew said, "since what we're about to tell you is off the record and he doesn't need to know about it. For now."

Was she thinking out loud or were they all mind readers? Amber took a breath and forced the crazy thought aside. She needed to calm down and focus. "I understand."

"Buddy and I have contacts inside the department, and they've shared details with us that Captain Aldridge might not be ready to disclose at this time," Jess explained. "However, none of what we're about to tell you is breaking the law. We're only bending it a bit."

"I'm grateful for any insights into what the captain is thinking." The woman gave every indication of being on a witch hunt. Amber had pondered the possibility that this was the captain's opportunity to get back at the press.

Since taking over as head of Crimes Against Persons, she had been cast in a bad light more often than not.

"I've had the opportunity to review the findings by the evidence technicians," Jess began, "as well as the lead detective's assessment." She turned to a new page in her notepad. "The victim's home is meticulously organized and painstakingly clean. No journal or personal notes were discovered, but I've asked the detective to have another look for any items that may be connected to other ongoing or unsolved cases."

Tension coiled inside Amber. "You believe he may have been involved in some sort of illegal activity?"

Jess hesitated but only for a moment. "The china teacups found on his table were the only pieces in that pattern found in his home." She removed a photo from a folder and passed it to Amber. "I've blown up the photo provided by the lead detective on the case. Look closely at the pattern. Is it possible those teacups and saucers came from your home?"

Amber studied the image, and her breath caught. She hadn't been able to see the pattern very well in the photos Teller had shown her. "This is my grandmother's china." Her heart pounded. "He or someone he knew was in my house." *Maybe more than once*, she realized as she thought of the knife.

Jess nodded. "Now we're getting somewhere."

Amber looked from Jess to the photo and back. "What does this mean?"

"It means," Sean interjected, drawing her attention to him, "that *you* have been a victim without even knowing it."

He was right. She'd been so focused on finding something that would prove she was telling the truth that she hadn't considered herself a victim.

"Kyle Adler may have been obsessed with you," Jess explained. "He may have come into your home on numerous occasions. He has no criminal record, but we're operating under the assumption that he simply hadn't been caught. His need to have something of yours may have caused him to cross the line, ultimately perhaps drawing him into association with the person who murdered him."

Amber looked from Jess to Sean and back. "So it's possible his killer may have saved my life. Is that what you're suggesting?"

"In some perverted way perhaps," Jess agreed. "Envy may have driven him or her.

The unknown subject—unsub—may have been Adler's lover who learned of his obsession with you and killed him in a fit of rage. When your name and face hit the news as a person of interest in the case, this person may have put the knife in your house to further implicate you as the murderer. Or if he or she was working with Adler all along, the knife may have been in your home since the day it was used as a murder weapon."

"How could he or she have known I would look in that particular box?"

"The choice was too specific to believe it's a mere coincidence," Jess agreed. "At this point my opinion would be that the unsub took his time and selected a place that wouldn't be too obvious to the police but wouldn't go unnoticed by you. Does anyone else know about the box of fan mail you keep in your closet?"

Amber started to say no, but the memory of the special she and Gina had done stopped her. "Gina and I did a special." She looked at Sean. "I told you about it earlier." To Jess she said, "We both shared a little about how our professional and personal lives intersect. I talked about the letters and…" Amber sighed. "And how I kept them in a lovely box on a shelf in my closet."

Jess nodded. "He was watching. He's using all he knows about you to frame you for murder."

"He's certainly done a top-notch job so far." Every piece of evidence in the case pointed to her as the murderer. How could her entire life be turned upside down in less than twenty-four hours?

"With your permission," Jess said, "the detective in charge of the case wants to have a couple of evidence techs go through your house a second time to see if they can pick up any overlooked prints left by the victim or any other potential unsub." Jess removed her reading glasses and placed them on her desk. "It's a long shot, but we shouldn't ignore the possibility that one or both may have been in your home many times."

Amber held up her hands. "I have no problem with them turning my house upside down if it helps find the real killer."

"There's always the possibility," Corlew warned, "they'll find more planted evidence that could hurt your case. You might want to run this by Teller before you commit."

Amber pressed her hand to her lips. She hadn't thought of that scenario. She shook her head. "I have nothing to hide. If something else has been hidden in my home, I want to know."

Jess nodded. "All right. I'll let Sergeant Wells know. She'll call Sean in the morning with a time."

"Meanwhile," Sean spoke up again, "I have a locksmith at your house changing the locks as we speak. As soon as we get back there, you should change your access code and your password for your security system."

Amber's head was spinning again. "I've never given anyone—not even my own parents—the access code or password to my security system. At least not that I can remember."

"There are other ways," Corlew assured her. "Perps can order electronic equipment on the internet that overrides or breaks access codes."

"Which is another reason," Jess cut in, "we believe the person who murdered Adler and planted the evidence in your home has done this before. He's too smooth to be a first timer."

Amber thought of the man Kyle Adler. She couldn't recall ever seeing him except for the occasional delivery. On those occasions he'd always seemed so kind and shy. His was not a face she would have associated with evil.

Sean spoke up again. "Does your station keep the original footage from your assignments or just the part that doesn't end up on the cutting room floor—so to speak."

"The station stores the footage that airs, but not the raw footage before it's edited." Hope welled in her chest. "My cameraman may keep all the raw footage. I can check with him."

"If Adler was watching you," Sean offered, "we might find him in the crowd wherever you were reporting breaking news. It's worth a shot."

Jess agreed.

Amber couldn't believe she hadn't thought of checking the footage. She had to clear her head and focus. Her future depended on how this turned out. She could spend the rest of her life in prison or end up on death row. Worse, a murderer could get away with his heinous act.

"Go home, Amber," Jess said. "Try to get some rest, but don't clean your house tonight," she added with a smile.

"Don't worry." Amber stood. "I won't touch anything I don't have to touch."

"Good idea," Jess granted.

As they left the building, Sean exited ahead of her. He scanned the street and checked his car before motioning for her to cross the sidewalk and climb in. He closed her door and went around to the other side. Dusk had the street lamps flickering on against the coming darkness. She closed her eyes and leaned fully into the seat. This day couldn't be over soon enough for her.

When the car moved down the street, she opened her eyes and turned to the driver. "Do you really believe we'll be able to find all the pieces of this puzzle?"

He glanced at her. "Don't worry—we'll find him."

Amber stared out at the darkness. "I hope so."

She didn't want the next story about a person who spent years in prison before being exonerated to be about her.

Chapter Five

Hugo L. Black United States Courthouse
1729 Fifth Avenue North
Tuesday, October 18, 10:30 a.m.

Sean did not like this one bit. He'd had no sleep since Amber had paced the floors most of the night. She'd insisted that was what she did when she battled insomnia. She'd also insisted he should take one of the bedrooms and just ignore her.

Impossible.

The loose fit of the pink flannel pajamas showed nothing of her curves or all that pale, creamy skin. There wasn't one thing sexy about the overly modest sleeping apparel, and still he couldn't keep his mind off her. At one point he'd even covered his head with the pillow. The move hadn't helped an iota.

He'd opted to sleep on the sofa since the layout of the family room and kitchen gave him a view of both the front and rear doors. The house was an older one, but it had been renovated at some point, opening up the main living space. The locks had been changed and her security system had a new access code and password.

First thing this morning she had informed him that she had to get back to work. She wouldn't discuss taking a vacation. She had ongoing assignments, she'd insisted. Apparently last night's insomnia had evolved into today's determination to pretend nothing had happened.

Three cups of coffee and one caramel latte later and Amber was rushing around the station prepping for the McAllister assignment. On the way to the federal courthouse, she'd explained that Forrest McAllister had been the go-to guy for investments by the who's who of Birmingham for many years. Eight months ago he'd been charged with insider trading. Now that same who's who were doing all within their power to distance themselves from the man. His trial started today.

Sean had heard something about the big

story, but he hadn't followed it. Apparently, he was going to now.

Watching Amber wasn't a hardship. The blue skirt and sweater she wore today fit her petite body perfectly. Her hair hung in soft waves, and those cute little freckles were faintly visible across the bridge of her nose.

Get your head back on the job, man. The cameraman had promised to dig through the work they'd done together. He couldn't promise he had anything Amber was looking for. Her first cameraman had retired more than a year ago. She hadn't been able to reach him yet. Sean intended to remind her to follow up with both men later today.

Vehicles sporting the logos of television stations and newspapers from all over the southeast ringed the block. Security had the courthouse locked down. The street, however, was brimming with people—mostly newshounds. Between the horde of reporters, the occasional helicopter overhead and the blaring horns of frustrated drivers attempting to navigate Fifth Avenue, the situation was a security specialist's worst nightmare.

There was no way to cover every direction from which trouble could come. He was left with no recourse but to stay as close as possible to his client. Sweat lined his brow. He felt as if he were guiding a rocker client through the crowd for a sold-out concert. It never ceased to amaze him how many megastars felt the need to brush shoulders with thousands of fans despite the risk that one of them might be a wacko. Sean had navigated the crowds, ever watchful and barely breathing. Like now. His senses were on full alert. Adrenaline had his heart in the fight-or-flight zone. Every muscle was tense, ready to react to the first sign of trouble.

The hearing had started at nine. Since the date and time of the hearing had been a closely guarded secret, the reporters following the case had missed McAllister's arrival. Word had traveled like wildfire as soon as the man was spotted entering the courthouse. Now they all waited for his exit and any sound bite his team of attorneys would permit to slip. Amber had managed a spot right up front, near the steps into the building. In the event of trouble, maneuvering through the crowd behind them would not be an easy task. Just his luck.

Suddenly, the towering entrance doors opened and a group of men exited. Sean recognized the main player from the shots he'd seen on the news and in the papers. The suits all around him were a combination of security and lawyers. The difference was easy to spot; the lawyers carried the briefcases while the others wore communication devices in their ears and constantly scanned the area around their client.

As if floodgates had been opened, the rush of reporters swelled into a tide of bodies, microphones and cameras. Sean wrapped his fingers around Amber's left forearm to keep her close. Intent on getting some word on how the hearing turned out, she ignored his move. Questions were hurled at the group exiting the building. Amber's was the loudest voice. For such a petite woman, she had a set of pipes and she knew how to use them.

The cameraman slipped in front of Sean, blocking his view forward. Sean held tighter to Amber and elbowed his way between her and the big guy.

Once the group reached the sidewalk, the crush of bodies was too close for comfort. Sean didn't like this. He angled his body to stay close to Amber. She stretched toward her target.

The huddle of security guards and lawyers abruptly stopped. McAllister stepped forward. A hush fell over the crowd of reporters. "Today was the first step in proving my innocence," he announced. "See you next week."

As soon as he was swallowed by his guards, the attorneys shouted, "That's all for today!"

Amber twisted to face her cameraman. "Did you get that?"

"Got it," the man fondly known as Bear assured her.

"Let's find a quiet place and do a lead-in," Amber directed.

Before Sean could suggest they get the hell off the street, she was climbing the steps to the building's entrance. She took a position and smoothed a hand over her hair.

"Hair and makeup are good," the cameraman assured her. "We are live in the studio in ten, nine…"

As he counted down, Sean scanned the crowd that had followed McAllister to the waiting limos. Behind him, Amber delivered a thirty-or forty-second overview of the case and introduced this morning's hearing results. When she signed off the air, Sean was able to breathe again.

The position they were in was far too open, not to mention they were backed against a wall—literally. No overt threats to Amber's life had been posed, but his orders were to assume the worst. If the attempts to frame her for murder failed, the perp might very well choose a different strategy.

"Can we get out of here now?" Sean asked as the cameraman packed up his equipment.

"We can." Amber moved toward him. "There's a clerk inside I want to follow up with first."

As long as they were off the street, Sean would be happy.

"See you at the station," Bear tossed over his shoulder as he hustled away.

Sean reached to open the door for her as a dozen or so of the reporters who'd only moments ago been hanging on McAllister's every move were suddenly closing in on them. He stepped in front of Amber.

"Amber, is it true the murder weapon was found in your home?" the nearest reporter shouted.

Sean turned his head and whispered to her, "Go inside. Now."

"Did they find your prints on the weapon?" another voice shouted.

"If you didn't know the victim as you claim, can you explain how this happened?"

"Were you and Kyle Adler having an affair?"

More questions speared through the crisp morning air. Rather than go inside, Amber stood stone still, staring at the people who were her colleagues—colleagues determined to get the story even if it meant turning on one of their own.

"What about those red panties they found in his bed?" a man accused as he moved to the front of the horde. "Are you going to deny they're yours?"

Sean didn't wait for Amber to react. He opened the door and dragged her inside. Two security guards immediately stopped them.

"We have a meeting," Sean announced, hoping Amber would snap out of her coma and get them past these guys.

"Paula Vicks," she said, her voice shaky. "She's expecting us."

After passing through security, Amber seemed to regain her composure. They moved to the elevators and she selected a floor. Sean kept his mouth shut as the car shuttled them upward. The elevators, like every other part of the building, would be monitored by security.

The elevator bumped to a stop, and the doors opened. She took a right down the corridor, and he eased up close beside her. "You okay?"

"Why wouldn't I be?"

He wasn't going to touch that one. "Good."

She seemed to square her shoulders as she

reached for the door. He followed her inside. A woman about Amber's age, tall and thin with blond hair and brown eyes, was waiting. She shepherded them into a small office and closed the door.

"I can't talk to you about the McAllister case, Amber. I can't talk to you about anything."

Amber appeared surprised. "What's going on, Paula?"

"Rumor is you're about to be charged with murder. I've taken too many risks giving you tidbits already. Anything or anyone related to you is about to come under intense scrutiny. I can't be a part of that. I'm sorry."

Amber nodded. "I understand. If you can just tell me the date of the next hearing on the McAllister case, we'll leave it at that."

"A week from today. Same time."

"Thanks." Amber exited Paula's office without another word.

Sean kept his mouth shut until they were back in the first-floor lobby. The tension radiating from Amber said loads. This ugly business had just trickled into her career. For a woman whose career came first, this new reality was devastating. Outside the reporters had thankfully vanished. They reached his car without incident.

Once they were inside, he asked, "Where to now?"

"My office. I need to dig up everything I can find on Kyle Adler."

"Then we need to go to Corlew's office instead."

Amber hesitated at the door he'd opened. "I thought your firm had already given me everything they had on Adler."

Sean shrugged. "You have everything obtained through the usual channels. It's time we checked out a few others."

When she didn't argue, Sean closed her door and rounded the hood. He'd call Corlew en route. If Corlew's contacts couldn't find it, it didn't exist.

The Garage Café, Tenth Terrace South,
11:15 a.m.

SEAN WAS NO stranger to the Garage, but Buddy Corlew considered the place his conference room. He held more meetings here than he did at the office. This particular meeting couldn't be held at the office anyway. Jess knew Buddy skirted the law from time to time, he'd done it for years as a PI before he and Jess formed their partnership. Jess, being the boss, had one rule: never break the law. So Buddy conducted whatever business Jess might not approve of here.

Buddy acknowledged their entrance with a nod. Sean ushered Amber to his table. She had asked a lot of questions on the way, and he'd assured her that Buddy could answer just about anything she wanted to know. Sean worried that no one was asking the right questions. To some degree the dilemma was understandable. At this point, the motive for Adler's murder was unclear. The motive for framing Amber was even foggier.

Buddy stood as Amber took the chair Sean pulled out. "I saw you on the news a little while ago." Buddy gestured to the screens hanging around the bar. "You think McAllister is innocent?"

Amber smiled, looking relaxed for the first time this morning. "I do not, but that conclusion is based primarily on the fact that I just don't like him." She leaned forward. "If you tell anyone I said that, I'll make my next exposé about you, Mr. Corlew."

Buddy held up his hands. "No worries here.

I've never met a woman who could tolerate a man who gave her secrets away."

"What about Kyle Adler's secrets?" she asked.

Sean wasn't surprised. The lady had built a career on getting straight to the point. He'd seen her falter a bit the past twenty-four hours, but she didn't give up.

"Mr. Adler was a strange one." Buddy rested his forearms on the table, leaning in a little closer. "He didn't go to college and still he was twenty-seven before he held a steady job and moved out of his parents' basement. He rented a small home over on Eagle Ridge Drive about two years ago. He made a living delivering *things*."

"Things besides flowers and dry cleaning?" Amber asked.

She stood by her certainty that the few times Adler had shown up at her door to make a delivery he hadn't come inside. Sean had pressed her to consider whether or not she'd ever turned her back for even a few moments. Had she gone to get a tip from her purse in the other room? Even a couple of minutes could have given him the opportunity he needed to make a move.

"Groceries, prescriptions, flowers, dry cleaning, you name it," Buddy said in answer to her question. "Your books overdue at the library? Just give him a call, and he would pick them up and drop them off for you. But he made his real money driving folks home from the clubs and bars around town."

A waitress appeared and took their orders. Buddy insisted they have lunch on him. Amber hadn't eaten that morning. After seeing what she kept in her fridge and cabinets, Sean expected her to order a salad. A woman as tiny as she was couldn't possibly eat more than a spoonful at a time anyway. She surprised him by ordering a burger, fries and a regular cola. Maybe she felt the need for carbs. He damned sure did. He'd been starving all morning.

"Did Adler ever drive you home?" Sean asked once the waitress was on her way.

Amber shook her head. "Absolutely not. I haven't spent much time on the club scene in years. Occasionally I meet friends or colleagues at a bar, but I always leave under my own steam."

Buddy pulled a folded piece of paper from his shirt pocket. "I compiled a list of the businesses he operated from the most frequently." He passed the list to Amber. "It's possible your encounters with him may have been more frequent than you realize. We shouldn't rule out anything. Start with that list and compile your own. Any deliveries, pickups, drives to the airport or to pick up your car after it was serviced, whatever you can think of that required assistance from another person."

She studied the list. "I recognize a number of these business. The dry cleaner." She pointed to another name. "The alteration shop. Still, I'm certain I've never seen him beyond a couple of flower deliveries and I think something from the dry cleaner's that once."

"We can't ignore the possibility that he disguised himself when he was delivering to you," Buddy countered. "You may not have recognized him."

"Oh." Amber frowned as she surveyed the list again. "I hadn't thought of that."

Buddy was right. If Adler was obsessed with Amber so much that he went to such extremes to be close to her, the possibilities for encounters were endless. "It's a little like looking for a needle in a haystack," Sean commented.

"It's a lot like looking for a needle in a haystack," Buddy agreed. "You just have to remember that the haystack can come apart the same way it went together, one row at a time."

"Has the BPD turned over any of the inventory lists of things found in his home or vehicle?" Sean looked from the list of businesses to Buddy. "It would seem to me they'd find the tools of his trade. Anything he used to get into houses like Amber's. Disguises, if he used them."

"Jess received a list from Lori Wells, the lead detective on the case," Buddy said to Amber, "but there wasn't the first tool or electronic gadget one would need for breaking into a house found."

Uncertainty nudged Sean. "Then he has to have a secondary go-to place. A storage unit or somewhere he keeps his gear."

"Or a somebody," Buddy countered. "The more Jess and I learn about this guy, the less we feel he was capable of anything worse than stalking."

"If we can't find the motive or the killer, the only way his murder makes sense—" Amber met Sean's gaze before shifting her attention to Buddy and going on "—is if we were friends or lovers and I killed him."

Her words hung in the air as the waitress delivered their drinks. When she'd gone, Amber continued, "The problem is, I hardly knew him. He's a face I barely recall. A smile of appreciation for a good tip after making a delivery."

"Did Detective Wells mention whether or not Adler had a cell phone and if they'd subpoenaed the records?" Sean suspected the BPD was already working on any cell phones and social media Adler used.

"They have," Buddy confirmed. "But it'll take a few days with all the hoops they have to jump through." He grinned. "I, on the other hand, have my own source. We'll have his phone records by morning."

"I'm impressed, Mr. Corlew," Amber said. "I guess Gina was right when she said B&C was the best."

Buddy gave her a pointed look. "First, no one calls me mister anything. It's Buddy. And second, just make sure you remember that my methods for being the best are trade secrets."

Amber smiled, the confident, relaxed expression she wore whenever she was on camera. Sean was glad to see it.

"You have my word, Buddy. I'm putting all my trust in you." She glanced at Sean when she spoke. "The two of you," she amended.

Sean would not let her down. He wondered,

though, if she knew the last woman he had
been assigned to protect and who had trusted
him had ended up dead.

Chapter Six

Amber wasn't entirely convinced about this route, but she had nothing to lose beyond a little time by taking it.

"Stick to your story," Sean reminded her. "Don't allow your emotions to get involved."

Amber's jaw dropped. He did not just say that to her. "Excuse me?"

How many years had she been reporting breaking stories? She'd waited for hours in the rain and freezing cold. She had followed leads into the darkest back streets and alleys of the Magic City. She had endured the latest trends in health, fitness and fashion. She never lost her cool or came unglued. Never.

At least not until today...

"You're a pro at digging into a story and

finding the details," he offered. "This isn't just another story—this is *your* story. It might not be as easy to do."

"I've got this." Not about to debate the subject, she grabbed her bag and reached for the door. She'd barely opened it and gotten out when he moved up beside her.

"It wasn't my intention to offend you," he said as they crossed the sidewalk.

"You didn't," she lied.

He opened the door and a bell jingled. Inside the smell of flowers overwhelmed all else. As much as she loved receiving flowers, visiting a floral shop was one of her least favorite things to do. It always reminded her of funeral homes and the day she'd had to go with her mother to select flowers for her grandmother. Amber shuddered. She hated this smell.

Sean leaned closer. "You okay?"

She flashed him a frustrated smile. "I'm fine."

Who knew how annoying having a bodyguard could be? No wonder celebrities were always coming unhinged in public. What kind of life was this? Someone watching every move a person made? Ordering that person around for her own good?

Then again, she decided as she reached

the counter, there was little chance of feeling afraid…or lonely. Sean Douglas paused next to her and sent her a sideways smile. Her heart bumped into a faster rhythm. Why in the world did her bodyguard have to be so damned handsome?

"Good afternoon," the clerk announced. "How may I help you?" She looked from Amber to Sean and back. "Do you have a special occasion coming up?"

Summoning her game smile, Amber glanced at her name tag. "Kayla, I'm Amber Roberts, and this is Sean Douglas. We're here to speak to Mr. Thrasher."

Kayla made an aha face. "Sure. He's in the back working on arrangements. I'll let him know you're here."

Amber thanked her as she disappeared through the staff-only door behind the counter. She'd researched the shop on the way here. Peter Thrasher was the owner. His mother had opened the shop forty years ago, nearly a decade before he was born. An old lifestyle interview from the *Birmingham News* during Thrasher's senior year in high school quoted him as saying flowers were his life. His mother had passed away the year before last. According to the obituary, she was preceded in death by her husband and Peter was her only child. If he had ever been married, Amber had found no announcement. Kyle Adler delivered flowers for only one floral shop, and this was the one.

The door opened once more and Peter Thrasher appeared. The six-foot-two man matched the few images she'd found in her Google search. His white button-down shirt sported the shop logo over the breast pocket. His brown hair was neatly trimmed and his brown eyes appeared overly large behind the black-rimmed glasses.

"Ms. Roberts." He gave her an acknowledging nod. "Welcome to my shop. How can I help you? I've just received a beautiful shipment of fall flowers. Gerber daisies, chrysanthemums and classic roses. I'm certain I have just what you're looking for."

"Sounds lovely." She reached into her purse and removed the photo of Kyle Adler she'd printed from her Google search last night. "I was hoping you could help me with a story I'm doing on Kyle Adler." She showed him the photo. "He was murdered a few days ago."

Thrasher looked from the photo to her. "I heard about his death." He gave a shrug, the gesture uncertain. "I also saw on the news that the police were talking to you about it."

"Did you know him?" Amber forged ahead despite the turmoil of abrupt emotions his words had stirred inside her. Maybe Sean had been right to warn her. This was not the same as chasing a story about someone else.

Thrasher nodded. "Not really. Not until he started his delivery service anyway. He was a friendly guy. Easygoing, quiet. It's a real shame, what happened to him."

"It really is," Amber agreed. "I want to do all I can to ensure justice for Mr. Adler."

Thrasher glanced at Sean. "Were you and Kyle…involved? I mean, after what I saw on the news last night…" His words trailed off as his gaze settled on Amber once more.

"I didn't know him. He delivered flowers from your shop to my home a couple of times. They were lovely, by the way." She searched Thrasher's face. "Did he ever mention me?"

Thrasher's expression turned defensive. "I see. You think he was some sort of stalker or obsessed fan."

"I don't think that at all," Amber denied. "I believe whoever killed Kyle is using me to get away with murder. I'm hoping that his friends and colleagues can help me find out who killed him."

"Isn't that what the police are supposed to do?" Thrasher stared at her expectantly.

Amber couldn't get a read on the man. Was he being indifferent or accusatory? His tone gave nothing away.

"Sometimes," Sean said, his tone undeniably pointed, "the police are too busy with other leads to see the real ones they need to follow. If you counted yourself a friend of Adler's, we're hoping you can help us find the truth."

"Anything you recall," Amber cut in, "might prove helpful. Did Kyle have any close friends that we might speak to?"

Thrasher stared at her for so long without saying a word, Amber was sure he wasn't going to answer. "Kyle was a loner. He didn't have any friends that I know of."

"How well did you know him?" Sean pressed.

Thrasher visibly withdrew. His shoulders went back and he eased a few inches from the counter. "I really didn't know him. He made deliveries for me. He was quiet and reliable. That's all I know. I have work to do, so if you'll excuse me."

He had already turned and reached for the door when Amber said, "You seemed disturbed by the idea that I might consider Kyle a stalker or an obsessed fan." Thrasher hesitated but didn't turn around. "If you didn't know him very well, why would that bother you?"

Thrasher turned back to face her. Whatever he felt or thought, he had wiped his face clean of any reaction. "I don't like the idea of anyone being made to look bad when he's not here to defend himself," he said, his tone barely above freezing. "Have a nice day."

Amber mulled over his words as she and Sean exited the shop.

"Strange guy," Sean muttered as he opened her car door.

She turned back to the shop before getting into the car. "A little."

When she was settled into the passenger seat and Sean had climbed behind the wheel, he said, "He lied about his relationship with Adler."

Amber had sensed that, as well. Thrasher's defensive reaction had been his only slip. "The question is, does he simply not want to get involved or is he protecting his friend by not revealing some not-so-flattering secret?"

"You may have missed your true calling." Sean grinned. "Maybe you're the one who should be a PI."

4:15 p.m.

"THAT'S IT." AMBER POINTED to the alterations shop. "Martha Sews."

Sean maneuvered into a parking spot. The alterations shop had a great location in one of the city's oldest neighborhoods that had gone commercial. Martha's shop was near Mountain Brook among a row of small houses converted to businesses whose front yards served as parking lots. Unlike the other shop owners, Martha had maintained the lovely flowering shrubs that lined the foundation of the house. With rocking chairs on the front porch, the place still looked like a home. Amber doubted the owner, who continued to live in the house as well as to operate her business, knew Kyle Adler any better than she did, but no stone could go unturned.

Amber sighed. She still found it incredible that the facts she needed to find were to clear her name. How had this happened? Her gaze settled on the driver as he shut off the engine. How had he handled the situation when his life was turned upside down? At some point she wanted to ask him about Lacy James. There had been endless speculation about the relationship between the star and her bodyguard in the media after her death. Sean had never acknowledged or denied they were lovers. Ultimately her death had been ruled an accidental overdose. But not before Sean had been crucified by the media. Unfortunately, being targeted by the media was only the tip of the iceberg where Amber's troubles were concerned.

"We going in or what?"

Amber blinked and turned away from the scrutiny of his blue eyes. "Yes." She grabbed her bag and reached for the door. As usual he was out of the car and waiting for her as she emerged.

He closed her door. She said, "Thank you."

As they moved toward the shop, rather than dwell on how Thrasher's slightly odd behavior had rattled her, she tried to remember all she could about Sean. She'd heard about his disappearance from Hollywood. At the time, no one seemed to know where he'd gone. She had vaguely wondered if he'd returned home, but then another local story had come along and she'd forgotten all about the disgraced bodyguard and the deceased pop star. Funny how fate had a way of bringing things and people back around. Maybe she'd have the opportunity to get the real story from him. His side should be told.

He reached for the door to Martha Sews but hesitated before he opened it. "I don't give interviews, Amber."

Clearly she was wearing her every thought on her face for all to see. It was the only explanation for how everyone seemed to read her mind lately. "I don't know what you mean."

"Part of my job is to recognize what a person is thinking before they act."

She would have disagreed with his conclusion, but he opened the door for her to go inside. It wasn't as if she could refute his statement. She had been wondering about an interview. She was curious about the man charged with her safety. His credentials should be of concern. Except he worked for Jess Burnett, and that said it all.

Annoyed now, as much with herself as with him, she struggled to pull off a smile for the lady who emerged from the back of the shop to greet them. "Martha, how are you?"

"I'm just fine, Amber. How are you this lovely afternoon?" The older lady frowned. "Were you scheduled to pick up your dress today and I forgot?"

Amber had almost forgotten the dress herself. "No. I think that's Friday." How had she let the dress slip her mind? She had a huge fund-raising event on Friday night. Assuming she wasn't in jail.

Martha nodded as she glanced at Sean. "It's always nice to see one of my favorite customers. What can I do for you and your friend today?"

"Actually..." Amber stalled. She surveyed the retail side of the shop. Martha sold all sorts of vintage items as well as one-of-a-kind scarves and handmade jewelry. If Amber recalled correctly, most of the items were on consignment. The extra income tided her over when the alternations were slow. Amber doubted that happened very often anymore. "My friend—" she wrapped her arm around Sean's "—needs a vintage bow tie for a fund-raiser we're attending."

"I see." Martha beamed. "Does your friend have a name?"

Amber put her hand to her chest, feigning embarrassment but also because her heart was suddenly and foolishly pounding after touching him. "Of course. Martha Guynes, meet Sean Douglas."

Sean extended his hand. "Nice to meet you, Ms. Guynes."

Martha blushed. "Call me Martha. Everyone does."

"Martha," he said with such charm that even Amber melted a little more.

"Let me show you what I have, Sean." Martha directed them to the far left side of the small shop, where ties and handkerchiefs stocked a vintage display case. She moved behind the case and slid open a door. "Do you see one you like?"

While Sean perused the bow ties, Amber said, "I was telling him you'd been in business more than a quarter of a century. Everyone who's anyone brings their alternation needs to you."

Martha gave a nod. "It seems like only yesterday that I was praying for some sort of answer from the good Lord. My husband had come home from a mission in the Middle East with undiagnosed PTSD. He drank all the time and was either deeply depressed and couldn't get out of bed or was on a rampage breaking things around the house." She sighed. "It was a hard time for me and our son."

Amber reached across the counter and touched her hand. "So many husbands and fathers returned with wounds no one but the immediate family could see."

Martha drew in a deep breath. "I was worried sick about just surviving. Since his troubles were undiagnosed, there was no money coming in. I had to find a way to make ends meet. I remembered back to the days before his illness when I would have coffee and play cards with the ladies from church. It never failed that when the holidays came around and folks needed costumes or clothes altered, Ruby Jean would say, 'Don't fret, girls. Martha sews.' I suddenly realized my old friend was right, and I opened this shop in my own living room. Here we are better than twenty-five years later."

"What an inspiring story," Amber said.

Martha shrugged. "We do what we have to do."

"I'll take that one," Douglas said, selecting a classic black bow tie that required hand tying.

"One of my favorites," Martha said. "It takes a man who knows what he's doing to get the bow just right."

"My father refused to wear a tie that came with a clip," Sean said. "I learned the art of hand tying at an early age."

"A sign of character and breeding," Martha said with a smile.

While Sean paid for his tie, Amber considered all the framed photos hanging around the room. Customers, including Amber, modeling Martha's work. Everyone she knew used Martha for her alterations. The lady was a household name.

"I was sorry to hear you're having some trouble," Martha said to Amber as she passed Sean a paper bag emblazoned with her sewing machine logo. "I swear, some reporters will make up anything for headlines. Anybody with one eye and half sense would know you wouldn't hurt a fly." She shook her head. "A disgrace, that's what it is."

Amber drummed up what she hoped was a passable smile. "Thank you. I'm sure the police will get to the bottom of what really happened."

Martha came around the counter and patted Amber on the arm. "You'll be in my prayers, hon."

"I appreciate that." Amber showed Martha the photo of Adler. "I know he made deliveries for you. Did you know him well?"

Martha considered the question before answering. "He was reliable. Pleasant. He went out of his way to be helpful." She shrugged. "I can't imagine who would want to hurt him. He was such a shy fellow."

"Did he have a girlfriend?" He may have been a very nice man, but her panties and her grandmother's teacups had wound up in his house somehow. Amber kept that part to herself.

Martha crossed her arms over her chest then and pressed a finger to her cheek as if contemplating the question. "I thought he was a bit of a loner. If he had any friends or a girlfriend, I never saw or heard about them. Why do you ask?"

The few details the police had shared with Amber had not been released to the press, which meant she couldn't share those with Martha. "Curious, I suppose. I'm hoping to find someone who knew him well."

"Are you doing a story on his murder?"

Amber shook her head. "I'm looking for the truth. And maybe a few answers about why I'm a person of interest in the case. Maybe he was an obsessed fan. I don't know. I feel like there's something the police haven't seen."

"You know," Martha said, "now that you mention it, I do remember him stopping once to watch you." She gestured to the small television that sat on one end of her counter. "He picked up the deliveries for the day, and he noticed you on the screen. He didn't move until the channel had returned to the regular program."

"Do you recall when this happened?"

Martha shook her head. "I'm sorry. I don't remember. A few weeks or so ago."

"You're certain he never mentioned any friends or places he frequented?"

"I think he played video games," Martha offered. "He brought my son a new game now and then." Her smile returned. "I think they spoke the same language when it came to video games."

"How is Delbert?" Amber felt terrible she'd forgotten to ask Martha about her son. Delbert was wheelchair bound and very reclusive. His father had died in a car crash and then poor Delbert had been paralyzed in a football injury. Keeping a roof over their heads and food on the table were only parts of the burden Martha carried. Caring for a physically challenged child was incredibly difficult to do alone. Few could handle the stress, much less the workload of operating a thriving alterations shop.

"He's doing well—thank you for asking. These days he helps me remember where I leave things and what I'm supposed to be doing. I'd be awfully lonesome without him."

"Does Delbert know his friend is dead?"

"We talked about it. He'll be a little more withdrawn than usual for a while." She sighed. "I'll just have to find another way to keep him entertained. Would you like to say hello? He'd be thrilled to see you. That boy thinks you're the prettiest thing."

Amber smiled. "I'd love to say hello."

Martha ushered them through her kitchen, where the scent of something wonderful emanated from the Crock-Pot. The house had originally been a three bedroom, but Martha had turned the larger of the three into a family room since the living room and dining room were lost to the business.

Delbert sat in his wheelchair in front of the television, his focus on winning the game playing out on the screen. The cozy room had Martha's touches all over it. Crocheted throws and framed needlepoint art. Amber often wondered if sewing was Martha's way of escaping reality. Everyone needed an outlet.

"Delbert, look who stopped by to see you," Martha cooed.

Her son looked up, his attention shifting to Amber. He smiled.

Amber moved closer to him and crouched down to his eye level. "One of these days I need to learn to play that game." She couldn't remember the name of it, but it was all the rage with gamers.

Delbert glanced from her to Sean. His smile faded, and he shut off the game and stared at the floor.

After several moments of silence, Martha offered, "We'll let you get back to your game."

"I'll see you next time, Delbert," Amber promised. Back in the shop, she said, "I hope Sean's presence didn't upset him."

"He'll be fine." To Sean, Martha said. "He's just not very good with strangers."

Delbert's story was such a sad one. Not long after the paralyzing injury he'd tried to take his own life with a drug overdose. He'd survived but the close encounter with death had left him with some amount of brain damage.

"I understand. I was in his territory. By the way," Sean went on, "do you know the name of the video game store where Mr. Adler shopped?"

"That place over on Riverview Parkway, I believe."

"Game Master?" Sean asked.

Amber was glad he knew about game shops. She knew nothing about video games and had no desire to learn. Several of her friends knew the lingo and all the newest games. They warned Amber that when she had kids she would have to learn. Since she had no prospects—even if she were interested—in a relationship, she doubted there would be children. Her gaze lingered on Sean. Did he want kids?

Where in the world had that thought come from? Had to be the stress. Her mind was playing games with her.

"That's the one," Martha confirmed. "I remember the bags." She frowned. "Do you think I should call that detective who questioned me and tell her about Kyle bringing those games to Delbert?"

"It could be significant," Amber advised. At this point anything could be significant. "We should be going. We've taken up too much of your time. I hope you'll call me if you think of anything else that might help us learn more about Mr. Adler's life."

"Of course." Martha shook her head. "It's such a senseless tragedy."

Amber prayed one tragedy didn't become two. One way or another they had to find Kyle Adler's killer.

When they were back in Sean's car and he'd driven out of the parking lot, he turned to Amber. "What's the story on her son?"

Amber gave him the details Martha had

given her after they became friends. "He's completely reliant on his mother."

"I guess that takes him out of the suspect pool."

No kidding. "I can't see Delbert as a suspect even if his physical and mental challenges didn't exist." These were people Amber had known for years.

"You see—" Sean glanced at her "—that's where you'd fall down in your investigation."

She shook her head. "What're you talking about? What motive could that boy possibly have?"

"First, he's not a boy. He's a man. And just because he's in a wheelchair and dependent on his mother doesn't mean he doesn't think like a man."

"Okay. How is that motive?"

"It isn't, but *you* are."

Now she was totally confused.

"He lit up like a Christmas tree when he saw you," Sean explained. "His own mother said he adores you."

Amber frowned, understanding dawning. "Then he withdrew when he saw you."

"He also shut off his game. He didn't want to share anything with me. He closed me out."

"Are you really suggesting Delbert is a suspect?" *Please.* There was no way. Even if he did think like a man where she was concerned.

Sean flashed her a lopsided grin. "I'm just pointing out how easy it is to miss clues when you're emotionally involved. Like Mrs. Guynes's comment about Adler being shy. Still waters run deep."

"Point taken." Amber tamped down her frustration. She'd thought the same thing about Adler. Just another reminder that the face of evil rarely looked the way one expected. "What we do know is that according to the police report there was no evidence of forced entry, which suggests Adler knew his killer."

"I found no signs of forced entry at your place." Sean glanced at her again. "Someone still got in and left that bloody knife in your fan mail box for you."

"Good point." Amber stared out the window. "If the police don't find the killer, how will I prove I didn't do this?"

Sean braked for a light and settled his blue gaze on her once more. "More important, how will you ever be safe if we don't find the person who did this?"

Amber's hand went to her lips. He was right. As much as she wanted to pretend this tragedy wasn't about her, somehow it was. She was part of the motive that had caused Kyle Adler's death.

"Let's go back to who might want to hurt you," Sean suggested. "And how that person could connect to Kyle Adler."

Amber wished she knew.

THE VIDEO GAME store proved a waste of time. No one who worked there recognized Adler. Defeat had set in nice and deep by the time they pulled into her driveway. Amber stared at the house where she'd felt safe as far back as she could remember. The kitchen had always smelled of fresh-baked cookies. Her grandmother had made her feel as if this house were her home away from home.

How could she ever feel that way again knowing a killer had been in her house…had touched her things?

Would there be Channel Six viewers out there—or maybe even friends—who would forever believe she'd had something to do with this man's murder?

She felt as if some part of her identity had been stolen, leaving a hole she might not be able to repair as easily as Martha mended a failing hem or split seam. No matter that she was twenty-eight years old, she suddenly wished her parents were in town. She'd insisted they not rush back. If they learned about the knife, they would be very upset. She'd have to make sure Barb didn't tell them.

"Is it your birthday or something?"

Her gaze followed Sean's, landing on the vase of flowers waiting on her porch. "No." She started around the hood of the car, but he moved in front of her.

She waited at the bottom of the steps while he inspected the large bouquet of red roses. Who would send her roses? If they weren't from her parents, she had no idea. Though she couldn't fathom her parents finding now a good time to send her flowers. The station? A fan? She went to a great deal of trouble to ensure most of her personal information, including her address, was kept private.

Sean removed the small envelope from the bouquet and opened it. He read the card and then showed it to her. "Looks like you have another admirer."

I'm watching you.

The stamp on the back of the envelope was the Thrasher flower shop. Amber checked the time on her cell. "We might be able to get back there before the shop closes."

"Let's bag the card before we do anything else."

Amber hurried into the house and returned with a sandwich bag. "We have to hurry."

"Dodging traffic is one of my finer talents," he assured her as he carefully bagged the card and tucked it away.

When they were settled in the car and he'd started the engine, he glanced at her before taking off. "You might not want to watch."

Deciding to take him at his word, Amber closed her eyes. Unfortunately, the terrifying images her mind conjured about the man who'd been murdered and the one who'd been in her house—perhaps more than once—proved utterly disturbing.

Sean was right. A connection of some sort existed between her and Kyle and maybe between her and his killer. How on earth did she find it? She'd done enough investigative reporting to know if a person didn't want to be found, they wouldn't be. A serial killer might use the same MO repeatedly and get away with it because he was too careful, too meticulous to leave even trace evidence.

Sean was right about that, too. In a case like this, the only way to find the killer was to find the motive for the murder.

Chapter Seven

Fourth Avenue North, 6:00 p.m.

The visit to the floral shop had been pointless. Sean had pushed Thrasher as far as he could without a badge and a warrant. The flowers had been ordered online, paid for with a gift card. The payment method was a dead end. It would take a warrant and considerable effort to trace the IP address of the computer used for the purchase. None of that was necessary in Sean's opinion. Whoever killed Adler had ordered the flowers the day before he was murdered with instructions they were to be delivered on this date.

The cops would see that element as proof Adler had ordered the flowers. In Sean's opinion the date the flowers were ordered didn't change the fact that Adler likely had a partner in whatever weirdness he was into. And that partner was in all probability his killer. Sean's conclusion confirmed the concept that Amber Roberts was in no way connected to the murder of Kyle Adler. She was a victim. All he had to do now was turn the card with the ominous message over to the BPD. Detective Lori Wells would follow up.

The boss called as they left the floral shop. Evidently the BPD had uncovered new evidence and wanted to meet with Amber. The drive to the office was tense. He could feel Amber growing more anxious. As soon as they arrived, he passed the card he'd bagged to Jess, told her about the flower delivery and brought her up to speed on the rest.

Ten minutes later they were still waiting in the conference room. Amber sat next to Sean. She kept fidgeting with her bag or the hem of her skirt. She was nervous, but Sean wasn't worried about her going down for Adler's murder. It didn't take a detective's shield to see she was being framed. Whatever the motive, the killer wanted Amber to suffer this roller-coaster ride or worse. It was the *worse* part that worried Sean.

Unless the detectives had found more evidence that would connect to the perp, he'd get away with murder. Why risk being caught by sending flowers to Amber? If eliminating Adler had been the goal, why continue taking risks?

"Sergeant Wells and Lieutenant Harper should be here anytime now," Jess announced, breaking the thick silence.

"You have no idea what this new evidence is?" Frank Teller asked.

Sean glanced to the other side of Amber, where Teller sat, his fingers drumming on the table.

"We'll all know soon enough what they've found," Jess assured him.

Sean liked his boss even if he wasn't so sure whether she liked him or not. He'd never met anyone quite like her. She was smart and brave. As far as he could tell, she wasn't afraid of a damned thing. She and Corlew were a strange combination. Both determined to get the job done but with different perspectives and from different avenues. Corlew didn't blink at crossing the line if that was what it took. *Oil and water*, Sean decided. Yet somehow they meshed. There was a long history between the two. One of these days Sean was going to ask Corlew about it. Maybe over a beer.

A bell jingled and the sound of Corlew's

deep voice filled the lobby, followed by Lori Wells's laughter and Chet Harper's quiet response to whatever Corlew had said. The two detectives were part of the family, Jess told Sean frequently. Along with Clint Hayes, Chad Cook and Corlew's wife, Sylvia. More of those close ties, bound by history. Sean wondered if he would ever again have those beyond his immediate family. The fact that his gaze moved to Amber at the thought made him want to kick his own backside.

The truth was, he'd thought he was ready for a lifetime commitment back in LA. He'd had the woman, the friends and the job. Life had been damned good. His life-shattering mistake had sent his friends running. The great job went next. The ties fell apart.

Maybe it was better not to get tangled up in close ties. No worries about being let down if you kept your expectations low. His gaze drifted to Amber. He didn't need complications like her, either. Getting involved with a client was always a bad idea. He'd learned that lesson the hard way.

Corlew and the detectives entered the room and settled around the table. Sean nodded to Lori and Harper. Since they all knew each other there was no need for introductions.

"What is it that couldn't wait until morning, Detectives?" Teller steered the conversation to business with his usual dry style.

Lori placed a folder on the table. She removed two photographs and passed them around. "Meet Rhiana Pettie and Kimberly McCorkle."

Both women looked to be twenty-five to thirty; Pettie was a blonde, and McCorkle was a brunette. Sean passed the photos on to Jess.

"Both are deceased," Harper said. "Strangled. Ligature marks indicate they were held captive for several days before being strangled. No indication of sexual assault."

"These two victims are related to our case how?" Jess asked as she handed the photos to Teller.

"We believe both women were victims of Adler and whoever killed him," Lori said.

Next to him, Amber drew in a harsh breath. Sean resisted the urge to reach for her hand and give it a squeeze.

Lori withdrew more photos and passed them on. "We located a storage unit near Riverview Parkway rented under Adler's name. Inside were three small plastic boxes. The kind you'd purchase to store a pair of shoes." She used her hands to indicate the size. "In each box was a pair of panties. A single pubic hair as well as one from the scalp was folded into each. Analysis confirmed the respective hairs belonged to the two victims." She indicated the photos that had made their way back around to Harper. "Along with Pettie's panties was a wineglass. The lab confirmed her prints were on the glass. In the box with McCorkle's was a coffee mug bearing her prints."

"Like my teacup and…"

Amber didn't have to say "red panties." Sean had struggled to keep images of her wearing nothing but those panties out of his head more than once.

Lori nodded in answer to Amber's unfinished question.

"Where were the bodies found and how were they dumped?" Jess asked.

"Pettie was taken Valentine's Day. She left work and never made it home. Her body was found a week later in the woods off Highway 280. McCorkle disappeared on June 20. Same scenario. She left work and wasn't heard from again until her body was discovered in a drainage ditch in Bessemer ten days later. Both were dressed in skimpy lingerie. McCorkle was still bound by the thin nylon rope used to secure her. Lengths of the rope were secured to each wrist like a bracelet. The one from Pettie's right wrist was missing."

Harper pulled yet another photo from the folder. This one showed a piece of blue nylon rope. "Considering this new evidence, we did another sweep of Adler's house. We found the rope tucked inside a family photo album."

"Did you find anything else like this?" Jess asked as she spread the photos of the items found on the table.

"We took his house apart," Lori answered. "We didn't find any other evidence anywhere on the property."

Jess removed her eyeglasses. "Ladies and gentlemen, we're looking at the work of a fledgling serial killer or killers. The MO is the same, though things were a bit sloppier with Pettie. The killer or killers had cleaned up their act a bit by the time they murdered McCorkle." She turned to Amber. "If I'm right, you were supposed to be the next victim."

Amber eyes widened. The pulse at the base of her throat fluttered. "Oh, my God."

"The third box found in his storage unit was empty," Lori explained. "The items belonging to you would have likely ended up there if Adler hadn't been murdered."

"We're assuming he was working with a

partner," Harper said. "And that partner killed him and planted the evidence to point to Ms. Roberts. We just don't know why yet. We also can't say whether Adler was involved in the murders."

"Does that mean my client is no longer a person of interest in the case?" Teller demanded.

"We have every reason to believe," Lori explained, "Ms. Roberts had nothing to do with Adler's murder. But until we know more she's still a part of this case."

"But she has been cleared of suspicion—is that correct?" Teller pressed.

"She has been cleared of suspicion," Harper confirmed. "At this point, we believe she may be in danger from whoever Adler was working with."

"Crimes Against Persons is officially handing off the case to the Special Problems Unit," Lori explained. "Captain Aldridge is not happy about it since the search she ordered turned up significant evidence, but the chief called it a couple of hours ago. Chet will be in charge of the case now."

"Excuse me." Amber stood and hurried from the room.

Sean followed. She went into the restroom, and he waited in the hall. As grateful as he was certain she felt to be cleared of suspicion, the other news had been startling.

Learning you were the next victim on a serial killer's hit list wasn't exactly like being named prom queen.

At least now he knew what the *worse* part was.

AMBER LET THE faucet run until the water was as cold as it was going to get, and then she bent forward and splashed it on her face. She gripped the sink to keep herself steady.

The dead man, Kyle Adler, had come into her home and taken her things. He could have touched any or all of her possessions.

Fear twisted inside her, churning in her stomach.

He'd taken her panties into his bed and fantasized about...*her.*

He'd wanted to kill her.

He'd probably killed or been a party to the murders of those other two women.

Amber drew in a shuddering breath as she stared at her reflection. She had been next.

Another deep breath and then another. *Calm down.* She needed to get back in there and hear the rest.

Reaching for a paper towel, she braced her

hip against the sink. She patted her face and dried her hands. She could do this. Adler was dead. He couldn't hurt her or anyone else now.

Except he had a partner…who'd in all probability been in her house, too.

Amber tossed the damp paper towel and opened the door.

Sean was waiting for her. "You okay?"

She pushed a smile in place. "I'm many things, but okay is not one of them at the moment."

He gestured for her to go ahead of him.

Amber squared her shoulders and returned to the conference room. She could do this. She was strong, and she had a bodyguard.

Jess offered a kind smile as Amber took her seat once more. "We were just discussing that you and the other two—" she gestured to the folder on the table in front of Lori Wells "—have nothing beyond being female in common."

Amber listened, struggling to keep her face clear of the fear pounding in her veins, as the detectives, Jess and Corlew, discussed the facts. Pettie was much taller than Amber and a little heavier. She had been on staff at one of the city's prestigious law firms. McCorkle was average height with a tiny waist and extra wide hips. She was an architectural engineer at one of the city's top firms. They shared no physical traits, as Jess said, except being female.

"The common characteristic that drew Adler may have simply been physical beauty," Jess suggested. "Or personality. Possibly body language. Whatever the commonality, he was drawn to each victim."

Amber wanted to know more about the partner. "How does a team of serial killers work?"

"One is usually dominant," Jess said. "Adler may have been the scout. He observed the target. Perhaps even lured her into a trap. The partner may have been the one to decide when and how she died. He may have been the one to make the kill, or they may have taken that step together."

"He left no evidence?" Amber was aware there were criminals capable of operating without leaving behind even trace evidence, but she didn't want this killer to be one of them.

"None we've found," Harper confirmed. "We'll continue interviewing friends, relatives, associates—anyone who knew Adler."

Amber appreciated their efforts. She moistened her lips and asked the question ramming into her brain. "What do I do until you find him?"

"You take extra precautions," Lori said. "You watch every step you make."

"Sean will be assigned as your personal security for as long as necessary," Jess added.

The churning started in Amber's stomach again. She swallowed back the bitter taste of bile. "How long will it take to find him?" She knew they couldn't answer that question. She, of all people, understood how these things went. She closed her eyes and shook her head. "I'm sorry. That was a ridiculous question." They might never find him. She might never know the name of the man watching her...waiting for the perfect moment to act.

"We'll do all we can as quickly as we can," Harper assured her.

"We've already taken initial precautions," Sean spoke up. "New locks. New security codes."

Amber's attention drifted. How could this man—this killer—have been watching her and she hadn't realized he was so close?

Chairs scraped across the floor and fabric rustled. Amber blinked. The meeting was over. She hadn't even realized the conversation had ended. She stood. The detectives were assuring Teller they would keep in touch with any new developments. Jess was speaking quietly with Sean.

Amber pushed in her chair and picked up her purse. Corlew joined the huddle with Jess and Sean.

"Amber, don't worry." Teller moved up beside her. "Between Jess and the BPD, we'll get through this."

She tried to summon a smile, but her lips wouldn't quite make the transition. "Thank you."

Teller gave her a reassuring pat on the arm, and then he followed the path the detectives had taken. Amber took a breath and lifted her chin. She should call her sister and her parents and let them know this latest news before they heard it some other way. This was good news on one level, she argued with herself.

Sean and the others broke their huddle, all eyes turning toward her.

After more assurances from both Jess and Corlew, it was time to go home.

Sean surveyed the sidewalk and checked the car before allowing her inside. Numb, she settled in the seat. He shut the door, and she flinched. *Deep breath. They will find this guy.*

She should call the station manager and discuss the situation. Was her cameraman in danger working with her? She glanced at the man driving. He was in danger, as well. Her sister. Gina. Maybe it would be best if she took some time off work. Gina was a reasonable person. Hopefully she could convince Barb to stay away from Amber until this killer was found.

Amber stared out at the familiar landscape. The plan seemed like a good one. Reasonable.

So she was going to put her life on hold because some evil, twisted bastard had targeted her?

No way.

"I need to go to the station."

Sean glanced at her. "Did you get called in for an assignment?"

"No. The computers at the office are better for what I need to do."

He made the necessary turn for the new destination. "Would you like to let me in on what we're doing?"

She considered his profile for a moment. Strong jaw and forehead with a nice nose balanced perfectly between gorgeous blue eyes. She wondered how often he'd been asked why he wasn't on the big screen. He had the looks, the charm. He could have gone for an acting or a modeling gig. Amber dismissed the silly notion. Her mind was working overtime to distract her from the worry.

Rather than answer his question, she asked one of her own. "What did Jess and Corlew say to you after the meeting?"

He glanced at her. "Not to let you out of my sight."

"Really? I thought that was already the plan. Isn't that why you're sleeping on my sofa?"

"Guess so." His lips quirked with a need to grin.

He likely wouldn't find the situation so amusing if the shoe were on the other foot. Still, she couldn't deny that seeing his lopsided smiles and grins were almost worth the worry and frustration. Maybe that was an exaggeration. Just another indication that her mind was on overload.

"So, what's on tonight's agenda?" He shot her a look. "I'm not going to let you out of my sight, but you're still the boss."

Amber relaxed the tiniest bit and told him what he wanted to know. "We're going to find out all we can about those two women Adler and his partner killed. Those women and I shared some common trait or connection that drew Adler and his partner. We have to figure out what it was."

"We should get food," he suggested. "I work better on a full tank."

She hadn't even thought of food. She wasn't sure her stomach could handle food. Two women were dead, but Amber had survived whatever the bastards had planned for her. The least she could do was help find the other person responsible for their deaths.

Going into hiding wouldn't be fair. Rhiana Pettie and Kimberly McCorkle and their families deserved justice.

Amber had an obligation to help them find it.

Chapter Eight

Thornberry Drive, 9:05 p.m.

"You're sure you want to show up at someone's door at this hour and announce you might know who killed their daughter?"

The idea sounded much better when she said it. "I have to do something."

Was she being selfish? The McCorkles had waited four months to hear who had taken the life of their daughter; the Petties even longer. Still, Sean had a point. She couldn't just show up at their door and announce that she knew the murderer. Not to mention the detectives on the case would not be happy with her, and the last thing she needed to do was to annoy or enrage the BPD. Odds were, the lead detective in the case, Chet Harper, had already spoken to the families.

Still, Amber had to do this.

"I'll be subtler than that," she assured him.

Sean grunted in that way only males could, the sound a warning that he had his doubts. *Fine.* She didn't need his approval.

She hadn't been able to reach anyone at the Pettie home. Mrs. McCorkle had insisted she was happy to meet tonight. If Amber had a daughter who had been murdered, she wouldn't care what time of the day or night news came; she would want to hear it as soon as possible.

Sean parked at the street in front of the ranch-style home. "Just remember, Harper's going above and beyond to solve this case. Don't do anything to make them regret the extra effort to keep you in the loop."

"Is that what your boss warned you about after the briefing?"

He shifted his attention straight ahead, and Amber knew she'd hit the nail on the head.

"Something like that," he admitted.

"I would never do anything to jeopardize my relationship with the BPD or with Jess Burnett." As a journalist, she understood the value of the relationships she'd built. As her mentor, Gina had kept that golden rule in front of Amber. She was no rank amateur.

Sean flashed her one of those killer smiles as he opened his door. "Well, all righty then."

As usual he was at her door before she was out of the car. He surveyed the street and the homes on either side of the McCorkle home before ushering her up the sidewalk to the porch. Amber rang the bell and found herself holding her breath.

The door opened, and an older woman, fifty or so perhaps, with dark hair looked from Amber to Sean and back.

"Mrs. McCorkle?" Amber asked.

"You're Amber Roberts," the woman said. "I recognize you from TV."

"This is my friend Sean Douglas." Amber indicated the man beside her.

Mrs. McCorkle gave a nod. "Come in."

When the door opened wider, Amber stepped inside. Sean stayed close behind her. Maybe a little too close. The heat from his body made her tremble. *You really have lost it, Amber.*

"You're certain we're not disturbing you, Mrs. McCorkle?" The guilt was making an appearance. Damn Sean for making her second-guess this move. If she weren't so vulnerable right now, he would never have been able to accomplish that feat. Investigative reporters ferreted out information on cases all the time. It was part of the job. More often than not the police weren't particularly pleased, but it generally worked out to everyone's benefit.

The lady shook her head adamantly. "I want to do all I can to help find the monster who took my baby."

Amber understood. She glanced around the neat living room. Framed photos of Kimberly were everywhere. "Is Mr. McCorkle home?"

The older woman looked away. "He's gone to bed." She wrung her hands. "It's hard on him. Truth is, he drinks enough beer every night after work to render him unconscious by the time he goes to bed."

"We all have our own way of dealing with loss," Sean spoke up. "As long as it doesn't hurt anyone else."

Amber wondered what he had done to deal with the loss of his lover when Lacy James died. Had he struggled to sleep at night? Tried to drown his sorrows? Why was it she suddenly wanted to know all there was to know about him? Yes, he was the man tasked with her safety, but she suspected there was more to it than that.

Mrs. McCorkle nodded her agreement with Sean's understanding words. "I tell myself that every night." She sighed. "Sometimes I feel like we're muddling through some alternate reality. How can this be our lives?" She waved off the words. "Please, make yourselves at home. Would you like coffee or hot tea?"

"No, thank you," Amber said as she perched on the edge of the sofa. "Was Kimberly a hot tea drinker?"

The lady shook her head. "That would be me. Kim loved her coffee in the morning, iced tea for lunch and dinner was a cold beer. She allowed herself one or two each night, the same as her father. He always warned that overindulgence was a bad thing. But that was before..."

"I love the flavored teas," Amber said, keeping her tone light. "Paradise Peach."

"I guess I'm a purist. Earl Grey for me."

"Green tea chai for me," Sean tossed in. "Only I cheat—I buy the instant stuff."

The man drank hot tea? When he shot her another of those amused looks, Amber closed her gaping mouth. She would need to be careful around him. He kept her off balance, and he knew it.

Time to get to the point of this meeting. "Mrs. McCorkle, I believe the man or men who hurt your daughter may have been targeting me, as well."

The woman's eyes widened. "Has someone else gone missing?" Her hand went to her chest. "Mercy, I've prayed nonstop that he would be caught. I don't understand why the police can't find whoever did this. They were here this evening asking more questions, but they weren't giving me any answers."

"I'm certain they're doing all they can," Amber assured her. "I'm wondering if your daughter and I had any hobbies, shopping habits or interests in common. May we talk for a few minutes about the things she liked to do?"

Mrs. McCorkle's eyes brightened, but the perpetual sadness created by the loss of her daughter lined her face. "She always loved building things as a child. It was no surprise when she decided to become an architect. She took great pride in her work."

"What about her hobbies?" Amber reached into her purse for a notepad.

"She loved playing basketball," Mrs. McCorkle said, her eyes growing distant. "She played in high school, you know. No matter that she was a foot or more shorter than the rest of the team—she was a force to be reckoned with when she got her hands on the ball."

"Was she dating anyone in particular?" Amber asked.

Mrs. McCorkle shook her head. "She had a lot of friends and dates, but she didn't date anyone regularly. Kimberly said she was in no hurry to get serious. She was busy building her career."

Amber's instincts started to hum. "I can relate."

"Kimberly had big plans. She wanted to have her own firm one day. She was going to take care of me and her dad. She promised we'd never have to worry about anything." Mrs. McCorkle's lips trembled. "She sure saw to that. She carried a million-dollar life insurance policy. We had no idea until we saw the paperwork among her personal papers."

"Do you mind sharing the name of her insurance company?" Amber, too, carried a significant policy. The day before she'd started her job her father had insisted on a "business" talk. He'd urged her to be smart with her money from the beginning. Setting up a savings plan was at the top of his list. Insurance and investments were next. Six years later Amber was grateful for that talk.

Mrs. McCorkle told her the name of the company, but it wasn't the one Amber used. After half an hour, Amber learned that she and Kimberly had very little in common beyond their single-mindedness regarding their careers. As significant as that similarity was, their careers were so different Amber wasn't sure how that had drawn a killer's attention. The firm where Kimberly was employed was nowhere near Channel Six. Maybe they shared the same maintenance crew, or maybe Adler had made deliveries to both offices or to their homes. The architectural firm hadn't been on the list, but maybe that was only because he'd delivered there fewer times.

By ten thirty Amber realized the woman would have gladly stayed up all night talking about her daughter. She passed Mrs. McCorkle a business card. "This is my cell number. Call me anytime, day or night, if you think of anything you believe would be helpful."

Mrs. McCorkle saw them to the door. "I hope they catch him soon."

Amber squeezed her arm. "I'm certain they will."

When goodbyes were exchanged and the door closed behind them, Amber felt exhausted. The meeting had been far more emotional than she'd expected. She had conducted plenty of interviews with families who had lost loved ones, but somehow this time had been more difficult. Certainly it was more personal. Those people could have been her parents...

Sean abruptly moved in front of her. She bumped into his back. His hand went under his jacket where she'd seen the weapon stationed at his hip. She peeked around one broad shoulder and spotted the trouble. A man stepped out of the shadows.

Gerard Stevens.

Irritation seared through Amber. "What do you want?" She stepped around Sean, but he stopped her with one strong hand before she could move toward Stevens.

"So the rumors that Adler is connected to the McCorkle and Pettie murders are true," Stevens stated with a satisfied smile.

"You know this guy?" Sean asked, his fingers still biting into her arm.

"She knows me," Stevens mouthed off. "She knows me *very* well."

"Adler was stalking me," Amber said, anger building faster than she would have liked. "I'm considering an exposé on women who're murdered by obsessed men. You better watch out or you'll end up in the story."

"I'll nudge my contacts at the BPD and confirm for myself."

Sean was urging her toward the car.

"You do that," Amber tossed at the jerk before Sean ushered her into the car. Stevens had made far too many enemies at the BPD to have any reliable contacts left. He was bluffing. How the hell had she ever been attracted to the arrogant bastard?

Sean echoed the question as he drove away from the McCorkle neighborhood. "You dated that guy?"

"Once or twice." More like six times. She closed her eyes and shuddered at the memory of the time they'd spent together. The moment Gina had found out, she'd told Amber that Stevens liked to bed all the new female competition, and then he bragged to his male peers.

Gerard Stevens had been her one big career mistake. Cutting herself a little slack, she had been young and eager to make all the right contacts in the business. At the time Stevens had seemed like a great contact. *Live and learn.*

"I guess pretty boys like him attract lots of women."

Amber considered the remark as they drove through the night. For such a handsome guy, Sean almost sounded envious. She wouldn't tell him, but he was far better-looking and more charismatic than Stevens would ever be.

"Trust me—his ego is sickening. What you

see is definitely not what you get. As a date he's a massive letdown."

"Ouch," he teased. "Remind me never to let you down."

During the fifteen or so minutes it took to drive to her house, Amber weighed the few facts she knew. If Pettie had been a career-oriented woman, that could very well be the attraction the three of them shared. Still, the killer had to have come into contact with each of them somewhere. What places or people did they have in common? Mrs. McCorkle hadn't been able to provide much in the way of places her daughter frequented. She had promised to talk to some of Kimberly's friends and get back with Amber.

Now if she could just get an appointment with the Petties tomorrow.

Sean checked the street before allowing Amber out of the car. He ordered her to wait in the living room while he checked the rest of the house no matter that the security system had been armed. Honestly, she didn't see how celebrities lived like this. She would lose her mind.

"Clear," he announced as he returned to the living room.

"Great." She needed to think. A cup of tea

and some quiet time would hopefully go a long way in making her feel a little more in control of her life. "I'm having tea. You want anything?"

"I'm good." He peeled off his jacket and tossed it over the arm of the sofa.

Yes, she mused, he was very good.

"I have wine," she offered as she lit the flame under the teakettle.

"No drinking while on duty." He reached up and plowed his fingers through his hair. "I'll just take a quick shower while you have your tea."

She shifted her attention to preparing her tea and tried her very best to block the images of him naked beneath the hot spray of water. She was tired and confused and plenty worried. There was no other explanation for her sudden inability to think straight.

While the water boiled she went to her closet and put her shoes away. She stripped off her clothes and pulled on a pair of pajama pants and a tee. It felt good to simply relax. She washed her face and dabbed on her nightly moisturizer. Her mother had taught Amber from an early age how important the nightly rituals were. Her father had been the one to insist she set and maintain a workout routine. Her parents were health nuts, and she was glad. So many of her friends struggled with finding the time to take care of themselves in their busy lives. The routines her parents had instilled had become part of her day, so she didn't have to make time.

The whistle of the kettle drew her back to the kitchen. She gave herself a pat on the back for only hesitating a mere second or two in front of the hall bath door. The sound of spraying water had ceased. She could imagine Sean in there toweling off that muscular body. She sighed. Maybe she just needed the relief of thinking about anything else besides her current fears. Or maybe it had been too long since she'd bothered with a personal life. So many of her colleagues had the same problem. There just wasn't enough time to establish an upwardly mobile career and to have a life, as well. A few, like her, had abandoned the idea of marriage and children for the foreseeable future. Most, however, went the other way. She had no idea how people like Jess Burnett and Lori Wells juggled such demanding careers while raising children. Maybe it was time she asked.

While her tea steeped, she prowled through the cupboards until she found a package of her favorite cheese straws. With her teacup and snack ready, she settled on the sofa with her notes. Sean wandered into the room, but she kept her attention on the notes. From the corner of her eye, she noticed he'd donned the same trousers and his shirt was only partly buttoned. She refused to look directly at him. She certainly didn't need to see any part of that body uncovered.

She sipped her tea and nibbled on the cheese straws. A short list of potential places where she and McCorkle may have run into each other was easy enough to make. A few boutique shops that catered to the professional woman. The dry cleaner. The municipal building. As an architect, McCorkle would likely be in and out checking property lines and zoning ordinances. Amber followed court cases. She spent a good deal of time at or around the city offices. Town hall meetings.

The same possibilities were true of Pettie, as well. Since she had worked for a law firm, they may have been involved with the same case at some point. Amber didn't recognize either woman beyond the reports she'd seen about their abductions and the subsequent discovery of their bodies. But then, she was usually so focused on her assignment she often had tunnel vision.

If she could get her hands on Adler's credit card records, nailing down shops and restaurants he frequented would help tremendously. Corlew was working on the phone records. Maybe he could get the man's credit card records, too.

Amber blinked. Her cup found its way to the saucer hard enough that it was a miracle it didn't crack the fine china. Her mouth felt numb. She set her notes aside and tried to stand. Her legs were rubbery. Saliva leaked from her mouth. She wiped it away. *What the hell?*

"You okay?"

Sean stood beside her. She hadn't even realized he'd moved.

"I don't know. I feel…" She tapped her lips and tried to swallow all the excess saliva. She swayed, her shoulder bumping into his.

"We're going to the ER."

She stared at him. His words were not really making sense to her. "What?"

"Are you drinking the tea from the can on the counter?"

She nodded, or she thought she did.

He sat her down in the nearest chair and disappeared. Her stomach roiled violently. "You'd better get a bag or a bucket." God, her mouth felt so damned weird. Numb and yet burning.

Sean's arms were suddenly around her, supporting her. "Let's go."

Before she could respond or catch her breath, she was in his car. How had they gotten there so fast?

He handed her a plastic trash bag, and then the car started to move.

Amber closed her eyes and fought the urge to vomit.

"Don't hold back." His words floated through the darkness. "Try to get it up."

As if his suggestion somehow triggered a response in her belly, she hurled.

"Good girl," he praised.

Funny. It didn't feel good at all.

Chapter Nine

University of Alabama–Birmingham
Hospital
Wednesday, October 19, 3:15 a.m.

Sean's teeth felt ready to crack he'd clenched so long and hard. He'd only relaxed when Amber had stopped vomiting and started to get comfortable. Her mouth wasn't numb or burning anymore, and she could stand, walk and communicate normally.

"We believe whatever toxin you ingested has broken down in the digestive tract," Dr. Chaconas explained. "We've taken the necessary detox precautions and given you lots of fluids. Your vitals are good. I think we're out of the woods."

"So I can go home now?" Amber asked, her voice still a little weak.

Chaconas glanced at her chart. "I don't see any reason to keep you." He made a few notes on the chart. "Come back here immediately if you experience any more symptoms, and stay hydrated. Check in with your personal physician as soon as possible."

"Thank you." Amber accepted the discharge papers.

As soon as the doctor was out the door, Harper came back in. "Looks like you're going home."

"Thank God," Amber said.

"I know you've been through a lot," Harper began, "but we're gonna need to go through your house again—top to bottom this time." He glanced at Sean. "I believe it's best if you stay somewhere else until we determine if there're any other toxins in your home. We wouldn't need more than a day or two and we should know within the next forty-eight hours what was in your tea. Is that doable?"

"My parents are out of town. I could…" Amber began. She frowned as if attempting to decide what to say next.

"She'll be staying with me."

Sean was as startled by the announcement as Amber appeared to be. Harper looked from one to the other and gave a nod. "I think that's a good idea," he agreed.

Amber drew in a big breath. "Whatever it takes."

"Good. We'll be in touch with updates."

When Harper was gone Sean offered Amber a hand as she hopped off the exam table. She swayed a bit; he steadied her.

"I, ah…" She moistened her lips. "I should probably call my sister."

Sean guided her into the corridor and toward the doors that would take them back to the lobby. "I believe I mentioned that when we first arrived."

"You're going to say I told you so? After what I just went through?"

He opened the passenger-side door. When she was settled in the seat, he passed her his cell. "You make the call—I'll get you someplace safe."

Sean rounded the hood and slid behind the wheel. He told himself he was doing the right thing. She couldn't go back home. She was his responsibility. It was his job to keep her safe. B&C Investigations didn't have a safe house as of yet. There was no need to wake up Jess or Buddy at this hour. He'd made the right decision.

Amber spoke quietly to her sister. Her sister wasn't so calm. Sean could hear the concern in her voice as she demanded answers. Amber responded steadily. He had to hand it to the lady, she was a trouper. She'd puked her guts out and was weak as a kitten, but she'd hung in there. While she had been undergoing the barrage of tests, he'd called Harper and notified him of the turn of events.

He was confident in his decision to take her home with him. Then why the hell was his gut in knots? Maybe because the last client he'd taken home with him had ended up dead.

His palms started to sweat. His heart raced. Now that they were driving away from the safety of the hospital, Amber was calmer than he was and she was the one who'd been poisoned.

Sean tightened his grip on the steering wheel. *You've got this, man. Shake it off.*

"Well." Amber passed his cell back to him. "That went over like a lead balloon."

"Yeah, big sisters like to be called during the crisis, not after." Another one of those life lessons he'd learned the hard way.

Sean braked for the traffic signal. The street lamp chased away the darkness between them. Despite the unpleasantness of the past few hours, a faint smile tilted her lips. "I see. You have an older sister?"

"Five years older and fifty times smarter." He laughed. "In her opinion, of course."

"Which is the only opinion that counts."

A smile tugged at his lips, and he relaxed a fraction. "Definitely."

The city was quiet at this hour. Back in high school he'd liked this time of the morning better than any other time of the day. The night was over, but it wasn't quite daylight…a fresh start. Anything was possible.

He had clung to that motto all the way up to the morning—about this time—when he'd made the biggest mistake of his life.

Sean checked his mirrors once more to ensure he wasn't being tailed, then he hit the remote to raise the overhead door of his garage. Once they were inside, he shut off the engine and closed the door. He hopped out and unlocked the door that led into the kitchen.

Amber closed her door and leaned against the car. "I hope you have something I can borrow to sleep in." She pulled at her tee. "This is a little gross."

"I'm pretty sure I can come up with something."

Sean flipped on the lights as he entered the

house ahead of her. He didn't have a security system like the one she had, but he had something even better.

Rebel sat in the middle of the kitchen, staring expectantly at his master. The tan-and-white boxer turned his attention to Amber. Amber stalled.

Sean patted his leg. "Come on over here, boy. He's the friendliest dog you'll ever meet."

"He's big."

"He's a teddy bear. Take a break, buddy." Sean pointed to the back door. Rebel bounded to it and scooted out the doggy door. "Follow me," he said to Amber, "and I'll get you settled."

"Why didn't he bark when he heard us coming?"

"He knows the sound of my car." He paused at the door to the spare bedroom. "Trust me— if anyone besides me had come into this house, Rebel would have taken him down."

"Who takes care of him when you're not here?" She surveyed the room as she asked the question.

His home was a classic bungalow, not nearly as large as hers, but with a decent-size yard for Rebel. It was on a quiet street in a nice neighborhood. "My sister. She helps with rescued dogs. That's how I got Rebel. No one else wanted him since he's kind of big and he's a little past his prime."

"So you took him." Amber smiled, the genuine article despite how lousy she no doubt still felt. "I would never have guessed you have such a soft side."

"Do me a favor, don't tell anyone. It would wreck my image."

She held up a hand. "Your secret is safe with me. Besides, I'm expecting you to keep any and all descriptions of my projectile vomiting to yourself."

"No one will ever know," he promised.

"I could use a shower, the sooner the better, and something to sleep in." She tugged at her tee again and made a face.

"And bottled water," he reminded her.

She pressed a hand to her stomach. "Right."

Sean rounded up a couple of bottles of water, a toothbrush and a Crimson Tide T-shirt. Amber was already in the hall bath, frowning at her reflection.

"I look like hell."

He placed the water and toothbrush on the counter and passed her the tee. "You look damned good considering. If you need anything else, just let me know. I'm at the end of the hall."

She touched his arm, stopping him. Even through the fabric of his shirt the contact sparked the desire already simmering in his veins.

"Thanks, Sean. I'm really glad you were there to take care of me."

He nodded and headed for his room. He needed a shower, too. A long, cold one.

8:15 a.m.

AMBER STARED AT the broth Sean had prepared for her. "I'm sorry. I just don't think I can do this." She had no appetite. She felt like hell. Her stomach still felt queasy and crampy.

"Just following the instructions on the discharge papers." Sean sipped his coffee.

Amber groaned. He was right. She needed to follow the doctor's orders. Slowly, she lifted the spoon to her lips and tasted. Her stomach clenched, but she kept going. One spoonful after the other, until she emptied the bowl. She washed it down with plenty of water. When she was finished, she pushed the bowl away and summoned a smile. "I feel better already."

Sean gave that one-sided grin that somehow made him even more handsome. "Liar."

She laughed. "Yeah. I feel…" She groaned. "Quite blah and very grateful for your quick thinking."

He gave a nod. "It's nice to be the hero from time to time."

Amber studied him a long moment. He really was a nice guy and completely committed to the job. She didn't see him as the type to fail a client. There had to be more to the story. "You know pretty much everything about me. I'd like to know more about you."

His relaxed expression hardened the slightest bit. "You know all the important stuff."

"Wives? Kids? Significant others?"

"Nope, nope and nope."

"You've never been married or engaged?"

He shook his head.

"Long-term relationships?" She reminded herself to sip her water.

"A couple. Nothing particularly memorable." He stared into his coffee.

"What really happened in LA?" She snapped her lips together. She actually hadn't been planning to blurt out the question.

He studied her for a long moment before he answered. "I made a mistake."

"Yeah, that's what you said before, but I think there's a lot more to it than just a mistake." She smoothed a hand over her ponytail. She'd been too exhausted to dry her hair after her shower. Her only option when she'd gotten up was to restrain the wild mass of curls. "I just feel like I deserve full disclosure from the man who's seen me at my absolute worst."

His lips quirked with the need to smile in spite of that stony profile. "I guess you have a point there."

Anticipation zinged through her. "So, let's hear it."

"Lacy James was smart and talented. And beautiful," he said, awe in his voice. "No matter that I worked extra hard to stay focused on the job, I was mesmerized by her. She had this ethereal beauty and incredible depth of soul that no one ever saw onstage."

"She was incredibly talented and beautiful," Amber agreed, feeling strangely jealous of the way he described her. For the first time in ages she longed to know a man saw her that way.

"I'd been in LA for six long years. I was lonely. I'd dated plenty between assignments but nothing serious. I was almost twenty-nine and maybe I was feeling the need for something real."

Amber's stomach took a little dive, and she was reasonably sure it wasn't about the poison. She'd been feeling exactly that way—as if something was missing in her life. No matter that her career had taken off; something was still lacking. She needed more than work. More than coming home to an empty house and an equally empty bed. But how did she trust anyone with her heart? The world was so full of people who cared only for themselves. In her profession she saw so much *fake*—it felt impossible to sort the real from the make-believe. Oddly, this moment—this man—felt real.

"The next thing I knew we were...together." He fell silent for a moment. "She had a short break before the next leg of her tour started, and we never left the house. It felt exactly like what was missing in my life. It felt real and good, and I wanted it to last forever."

Amber watched the pain clutter his handsome face. The memories still hurt even though a year had passed. Was he still in love with her memory?

"When I was briefed on the assignment, her agent warned me not to trust her. She was never allowed to overindulge in alcohol, and if I spotted drugs, I was to get her out ASAP." His gaze met Amber's, and the agony there tugged at her heart. "Lacy was an addict. Had been since she was thirteen. When we met she'd been straight for two years."

"No one is responsible for what an addict chooses to do," Amber reminded him softly.

He nodded. "I know. But that doesn't change the responsibility I feel. I was with her 24/7 for weeks. I took my eyes off her for one minute at a party while she went to the bathroom and she scored. That night after I went to sleep, she overdosed on cocaine. She was sitting right there in the room watching me. I didn't even know she'd gotten out of bed." He stood and gathered her bowl and spoon. "That's what happens when you get too comfortable. Your sense of caution becomes dulled. You miss things. Lacy's dead because I didn't see how getting personally involved with me made her feel out of control. Made her wish for things she couldn't have if she wanted to keep her career on track."

"Are we all doomed to that choice?" Amber bit her lips together. She hadn't meant to say those words out loud. What was it about this man that made her feel the need to be so forthcoming? "I mean, can't a woman or a man have an astonishingly successful career and a personal life? Why do we have to choose only one?"

"There's a career," Sean said, his tone somber, "and there's a *career*. When you choose the latter, there's nothing else. It's all-encompassing. After the funeral, the one trusted friend she had told me I reminded Lacy how much she regretted the choices she'd made. She'd given up everything—her first love, the child they'd had together—to follow her dream. Falling in love again sent her hurtling back into the pain and loss."

Amber stood and pushed in her chair. "It isn't fair that she had to give up one or the other. Why couldn't she have had both?" Her heart was pounding. What she was really asking was why couldn't she have both? What made women like her—like her sister and Gina and even Jess Burnett—believe they had to give up a real life for their careers? Though the dilemma rarely affected men the same way, Sean seemed to be stuck in that same place.

"It took me nearly a year of soul-searching and no small amount of counseling to come to terms with the answer to that question, Amber. Are you sure you want to hear it?"

She blinked, taken aback. "Why wouldn't I?"

"Lacy couldn't have both because she was an addict. Staying completely focused on her career helped her keep it together—helped her stay clean. I disrupted the rhythm she'd come to depend on. I should have recognized the issue, but I was too infatuated, too caught up in my own needs. I failed to do my job, and for that I'm in part responsible for her death."

"Are you suggesting I'm addicted to my work? That I don't care about anything else?"

Sean exhaled a big breath. "I'm suggesting if you can't see yourself living a personal life in addition to your career, then you won't be able to have both. You'll have to choose one or the other, and there will always be regrets with whichever choice you make. Isn't that the true definition of addiction? Being willing to sacrifice everything else for the one thing you want most?"

The doorbell rang, and Amber jerked at the sound. "Barbara said she'd bring me some of her clothes."

"I'll get the door."

Amber took a deep breath and let it out slowly. Why in the world had they been discussing her love life and career decisions? It was her own fault. She'd started it. The conversation was meant to learn more about him and what happened in LA. It was never intended to dissect her life.

Could he possibly be right about her? Was she incapable of balance? She couldn't deny being singularly focused. She'd recognized her type A personality at the ripe old age of twelve. She'd decided then that she wanted to be the next Barbara Walters.

Barb's voice in the other room drew her from her thoughts. This wasn't the time to worry about her love life. Two women were dead—possibly murdered by the same man who had poisoned her. Finding Adler's partner and presumably his murderer had to be top priority right now. Just because Sean Douglas made her heart pound and her pulse skip was no excuse to revert to being controlled by adolescent hormones.

Amber squared her shoulders and joined her sister and Sean in the living room. Barb took one look at her and rushed to where she stood. She grabbed Amber in a bear hug. "Don't you ever do that again!"

Amber tried to breathe. Sean stood on the other side of the room, his arms loaded with clothes, shoes and a small bag hanging from his long fingers.

"Really, I'm okay," Amber assured her.

Barb drew back and surveyed her from head to toe and back. "You look like hell. You definitely need all that makeup Gina shoved into the bag the cutie-pie over there is holding."

Sean looked at the floor in an attempt to hide his grin.

"Thanks." Amber knew she was okay when her big sister told her she needed makeup. Barbara Roberts hated makeup. How she ever fell in love with a television journalist like Gina was a mystery to Amber. "The cutie-pie," she said, using Barb's term, "is Sean Douglas."

"A pleasure." Barb gave him an approving nod and grabbed the bag he held. "Come on, little sister." She reached for one of the outfits he held, as well. "We have work to do. You'll have to excuse us, Mr. Douglas."

"Take your time," he suggested. "I'll follow up with Lieutenant Harper."

Amber flashed him a smile as her sister ushered her from the room. What was it about a near-death experience that made a woman suddenly bemoan all she'd given up for a career?

How did she capture that elusive thing called balance?

As soon as the person trying to kill her was caught, she intended to find her balance.

She glanced over her shoulder one last time. Maybe she would start with Sean.

Chapter Ten

Frontier Drive, Vestavia Hills, 11:00 a.m.

Rhiana Pettie's mother had agreed to a meeting.

Amber looked considerably better even if she still felt weak and weary. Barb had helped her pull herself together. Her head was still just a little foggy, but an extrasweet café mocha had helped immensely.

Sean parked at the curb and checked his cell. "Harper sent me a text. So far your place is coming up clean for toxins, but he'd feel better if you gave them another day just to be sure."

"I can live with that." She searched his eyes. "Can you?" After all, he was the one sharing his place.

"My job is to keep you safe, Amber. I can do that just about anywhere."

"I guess it's settled then. I'll be at your place again tonight."

His blue eyes darkened. "Technically it'll be your first night at my place. It was already morning when I took you there today."

"I used your shower and spent time sleeping in your guest bed."

He nodded. "You did."

"I rest my case." Amber reached for the door. As usual, he somehow managed to appear at her side of the car before she emerged.

Forty-eight hours ago she'd found his persistent presence frustrating, annoying even. Now she was very grateful he was here. The reality that someone had come into her house and touched her things was bad enough. To recognize that he'd meant her physical harm made it all the worse. It was one thing to have an obsessive fan, even a stalker; it was entirely another to be targeted for death.

Amber turned her attention to the brick home nestled on the corner of Frontier and Kingswood. According to her research, the Petties had lived here for thirty-five years. Rachel and Tom, Rhiana's parents, had three grown children, but she had been their only daughter. People always pointed out statistics like those. If they'd had another daughter, would Rhiana's death have been easier? Of course not.

The door opened, and Mrs. Pettie stared at them as if she'd forgotten they were coming.

"Mrs. Pettie, I'm Amber Roberts. We spoke about an hour ago. You said my associate Sean Douglas and I could come by to speak with you about Rhiana."

She nodded and opened the door wider. "You look different than you do on television."

Amber relaxed a little as she crossed the threshold. "Most people say I look much taller on TV."

Pettie managed a faint smile. "I think they're right. You do look taller on-screen."

Rhiana's mother went through the usual steps, offering refreshments, which they both declined, and steering them toward the sofa. Pettie was tall like Rhiana. Her blond hair was more gray now than blond, but the resemblance to her daughter was unmistakable. Amber had inherited her red hair and green eyes from her mother. Barb, on the other hand, had inherited their father's rich brown hair and dark eyes. People who didn't know them rarely believed they were sisters.

"The police told me they may have found the man who took her from us."

Amber nodded. "Yes. I hope the BPD can confirm those suspicions soon. I'm certain they'll contact you again as soon as they do."

Pettie's brow furrowed into a frown. "Are you reporting on the investigation?"

Amber glanced at Sean. This was where things got a little muddled and a whole lot sticky.

"Mrs. Pettie," Sean answered for her, "the police have reason to believe Amber was the next victim on the killer's list. As you can imagine, she's anxious to help solve the case."

"Is that why they thought you killed him?"

Amber hoped that debacle wasn't going to follow her forever. "I was and still am a person of interest in the case, but the police have cleared me of any suspicion related to his murder." It felt really good to be able to say those words.

"Can you tell us about the last few days before your daughter went missing?" Sean asked. "Had she met anyone new? Was she working on a new case at the firm?"

Amber flinched. He'd gone straight to the point rather than easing into the hard questions.

"The police already asked questions about those days," Pettie said, her gaze drifting to the floor. "After she first went missing and then again yesterday."

"Sometimes it helps to have new eyes and ears on a case. That's why we're here," he explained gently.

Pettie cleared her throat. "Rhiana was a hard worker," she said softly. "She put in a lot of long hours. I cleaned her apartment for her every couple of weeks." She smiled. "I didn't mind. Anytime she was home in the evenings she had dinner with her father and me. I think that's what I miss most...doing things for her. I loved hearing about her day. She would share the details she could, and it was always so exciting."

The loss she felt thickened in the room. It was moments like this when Amber wondered how on earth anyone could bear to have a child. How did a parent survive losing a child? *Keep your attention on the goal—finding this bastard.*

Amber braced for a no. "Can we see her apartment?"

Pettie hesitated, but then she stood. "I've left it just as it was. 'Course, the police went through her room twice, but otherwise it's exactly the way she left it."

"We'll be very careful," Sean promised.

"Follow me," Pettie offered.

There was something immensely comforting about Sean's hand at the small of her back as Amber followed Pettie up the exterior stairs that led to the apartment over the garage. She unlocked the door and stood back for them to enter first.

Rhiana had a large space that included a small bathroom and kitchenette. It was roomier than Amber's first apartment out of college. She'd refused the offer to move back in with her parents. The tiny apartment had been her only option.

The pajamas Rhiana had slept in the night before she disappeared were on the unmade bed. The bowl and coffee mug she'd used that morning were in the sink. A large bouquet of dead flowers sat on the coffee table in front of the small sofa. Amber leaned down for a closer inspection. Roses...red ones, she suspected, though they had turned black, many of the petals falling to the table.

"She was excited about the flowers," Pettie said. "She thought the junior partner she'd been smitten with for a year had finally noticed her." Her face fell. "When he was questioned, he told the police he didn't send them."

"Were they delivered here or at her office?" Sean asked.

"Her office. She brought them home with her the same day she received them. She was so excited," Pettie repeated.

Amber's heart ached for her. "Was there a card?" She searched the area around the bouquet.

The older lady wrung her hands in front of her. "There was, but as far as I know the police never found it."

Rhiana had gone missing Valentine's Day, eight months ago. The chances of finding the card now were slim to none. Amber straightened. "Did someone from the firm send home the personal items from Rhiana's office?"

Amber felt certain they would have cleared out the office reasonably soon after the body was found. The law firm where Rhiana had worked was a busy one; up-and-coming attorneys and paralegals were essential to the fast-paced operation of the firm. Office space was no doubt a premium.

"One of her colleagues packed everything in boxes, and Rhiana's father brought them home." She sighed. "At the time I wasn't up to facing people. I think he put the boxes in the garage. That's usually where he puts everything." She glanced around the room. "I meant to bring them up here, but I... I never got around to it. We can go down and look for them if you'd like."

Amber and Sean followed Pettie down to the garage. Sean pulled the two boxes from the top shelf where Mr. Pettie had stored them.

"May we have a look inside?" Sean asked.

Pettie nodded. "Are you looking for the card that came with the flowers? I think the police went through her office and didn't find it."

"We know new details now," Amber offered. "Perhaps something else we find will mean more than it would have all those months ago."

Sean opened first one box, and then the other. Rather than being sealed with tape, each had been closed by folding the flaps one over the other. Careful with the items that had likely decorated Rhiana's office, Amber emptied the first box. Sean glanced at her, and she shook her head. Nothing potentially useful to the case.

Amber's hopes plummeted as the second box provided nothing relevant to the case, either. The last item in the box was a stack of business cards bound together with a rubber band. She might as well verify that the card wasn't among them. As she reached the final three, her fingers stilled. Holding one of the cards by the edges, she turned it for Sean to see. *Thrasher Floral.*

It wasn't the warning Amber had received, but it showed a connection to the same floral shop. The police couldn't have recognized the connection when Rhiana went missing.

"Mrs. Pettie, do you have a plastic bag we could put this in?" Sean asked before Amber had the presence of mind to do so.

The lady nodded and hurried into the house.

"We need to see Kimberly McCorkle's home." Anticipation seared through Amber's veins. They were on to something here. "If we can find even the smallest connection to the floral shop, we'll have something to take to Lieutenant Harper."

"We should call him first," Sean countered. "This is evidence."

Sean was a former cop. Amber understood his desire to be a team player—particularly since the cops involved were his friends. Unfortunately there wasn't time. A murderer—possibly a serial killer—was out there, and it was more than probable that he still intended to make Amber his next victim. Not to mention there were two families who desperately needed answers sooner rather than later.

Amber made up her mind. "We can call him after we see Kimberly's house."

Sean would have argued, but Mrs. Pettie returned with a sandwich baggie.

The memory of their rush to the emergency room when Amber had been poisoned surged to the front of her mind. She had to see this through. Now.

Beckham Drive, 12:45 p.m.

SEAN WAS SURPRISED when McCorkle agreed to meet them at her daughter's home without asking the first question. He parked in front of the small house near the popular Five Points district. The cottage had been a present to Kimberly from her parents when she graduated from college. Like Rhiana Pettie's apartment, the house had been closed and left just as it was the day their daughter walked out the last time—except for the official BPD investigation.

He didn't like doing this. Despite his misgivings, he climbed out and went around to the passenger side as Amber emerged. "You know Lieutenant Harper will be ticked off," he reminded her for the third time. He had no desire to step on the toes of the BPD's finest.

Jess would not be happy, either. But Amber was the client. Wasn't it his job to keep the client safe *and* happy? *Damn.*

"We will call him as soon as we're done here," Amber repeated the same response she'd given him last time he'd raised the issue.

He exhaled a big breath and followed her up the walk to the front door. McCorkle was waiting just inside. She opened the door wider as they approached.

"I was surprised when you called me again so soon." The older lady looked hopefully at Amber. "Does this mean new evidence has been found?"

Amber smiled. Sean should have looked away, but he didn't. Her smile was part of what had landed her in the television business, in his opinion. When she smiled, everything else faded into insignificance. She was genuinely beautiful.

No going there, pal. He'd spent plenty of time admiring her physical attributes before they even met. If he was completely honest with himself, he'd gone way past the admiration stage. He had to put the brakes on for now. Maybe when this assignment was finished…

Had he just made a plan to pursue something beyond work?

"We're hoping to find a connection no one knew about before," Amber explained as she glanced around the cramped living room.

Her words dragged Sean back to the here and now.

Like Rhiana Pettie's house, there was no security system, Sean noted. A small sofa and cocktail table were overpowered by a massive drawing desk and light. One wall was covered with bookshelves, but rather than filled with books, the shelves were stacked with rolls of architectural drawings. The shelves were labeled alphabetically.

No flowers in the living room.

"May we see the rest of the house?" Amber asked, her anticipation showing.

"Oh, sure." McCorkle gestured to the far side of the room. "The hall leads to the two bedrooms and a bathroom. The kitchen is that way." She indicated the doorway to the right. "The police moved things around a bit, but otherwise it's all just like she left it that last morning before she went to work."

A narrow pair of swinging doors separated the living room from the tiny kitchen. In the sink sat the vase of flowers. Adrenaline fired across Sean's nerve endings. It was way past time to call the cops.

Amber leaned close and visually examined what was obviously an arrangement of dead roses. She turned to McCorkle. "Do you know when she received the flowers?"

The older woman nodded. "The day before…"

"Did she mention who they were from or if there was a card?"

McCorkle shook her head. "She didn't. She only said that she was mad that he wouldn't let go."

Another blast of adrenaline nailed Sean. "Who did she mean? An old boyfriend?"

"Yes. They had broken up the month before, but he kept calling. The police interviewed him and eventually ruled him out. They said he had an airtight alibi."

"What was the ex-boyfriend's name?" Amber asked.

"Quentin Yates. He works for another architectural firm in town."

"Do you mind if we look around for a card?" Sean didn't wait for Amber to ask. As mad as Harper would be, this could be a major break in the case.

"I'll help you," McCorkle offered.

Since the flowers were in the kitchen, that was the logical place to start. The evidence techs had taken the garbage to the lab. Sean figured if they'd found a card with a sinister note, they would have marked it as evidence. Since that wasn't in any of the reports, he was going with the theory it hadn't been found.

When they had checked every nook and cranny in the small kitchen, they moved to the living room. Amber chatted casually with McCorkle. Sean decided she could have been a cop herself. She had a way of prompting answers without directly asking the questions. McCorkle didn't hesitate even once. Sean doubted she realized she was being interrogated. By the time they moved on to the bedrooms, Amber knew all about Kimberly's social life and the long, hard path to her career.

"I'll take the bathroom," Sean offered. He had no desire to spend the next twenty minutes or so trapped in one of those little bedrooms with Amber. In the past twenty-four hours she had gotten deep under his skin. He wished he could regret it, but the necessary emotion just wouldn't come. He knew it was wrong, but he couldn't help savoring it.

As good as it felt, it could not go any further while he was responsible for her safety. He could fantasize all he wanted.

Kimberly McCorkle's bathroom was crammed

with the usual female necessities. Lots of hair and skin products. Loads of fragrances. Various types of razors. Toothpaste. Bodywash in a variety of scents. Amber's bathroom looked a lot like this. The first night he'd stayed at her house he'd had a hell of a time evicting her scent from his system. The subtle citrus fragrance was fresh and clean and made him long to taste every inch of her.

"Idiot," he muttered. He moved on to the medicine cabinet. No drugs other than aspirin and a half-empty prescription of antibiotics.

"Sean!"

He closed the mirrored medicine cabinet door and hurried to the bedroom at the end of the hall.

Amber pointed to the jewelry box on the dresser. "It was under the velvet lining."

He moved to her side and took a look. Amber had removed several necklaces and a watch, as well as the lining in the bottom of the jewelry box. How had the evidence techs missed this? "Was it obviously loose?"

"No. One of the necklaces hung in the fabric and pulled it away from the bottom."

At the bottom of the box were a couple of folded notes and the card from the floral shop lying right on top. It wasn't a business card; it was the one sporting the note that accompanied the bouquet. *I'm watching you.*

"We need a plastic bag," he muttered.

"I'll get one," McCorkle said, sounding breathless.

Amber reached into the jewelry box and gingerly removed the card by its edges. "Should we look at the notes, too?"

"For sure." Sean removed the stack of notes carefully; there were four in all. Each was from the ex, Yates, who hadn't wanted to end the relationship.

"She thought the flowers were from him," Amber said. "She was keeping all this in case she needed it in the future."

But her future never came. The words echoed through Sean's head. Amber wouldn't have a future either if this bastard had anything to do with it.

McCorkle returned with a plastic sandwich bag and Sean bagged the evidence. Amber made her aware of the notes, which weren't particularly threatening, simply obsessive. Sean's mind wouldn't quit replaying those haunting words.

Did Amber have any idea how lucky she was to be alive? His throat tightened.

By the time they were at the front door, McCorkle's composure had frayed.

"We'll get this evidence to the police," Sean assured her. "They'll get this guy."

When they were in the car and headed downtown, Amber turned to him. "Before we go to the police, I want to go back to the floral shop."

Sean moved his head firmly side to side. "No way."

"It can't be a coincidence that all three flower arrangements came from the same florist and that at least two had the same warning."

Sean wouldn't deny the point. "It's still circumstantial and—" he shot her a pointed look "—we're playing fast and loose with evidence that may prove necessary to solving a double homicide."

She twisted in the seat and pled her case from a different perspective. "We have no idea what this guy does to stay ahead of the police. We do know he got past my security code. He could be listening to a police radio. I don't want him tipped off."

Sean shook his head. He had to be nuts, and yet she had a point. "What do you expect to say to Thrasher?"

She sighed. "I don't know. All I know for sure is that I don't want him to get away."

Sean braked for a light, and she touched his arm. He turned to her, and the stark fear on her face startled him. "How will I ever feel safe again if he gets away?"

Before he could stop the words, he made a promise he hoped like hell he could keep. "I won't let that happen."

Chapter Eleven

Thrasher Floral, Pearson Avenue, 3:00 p.m.

"Can we go in now?" Amber asked again.

Sean didn't like the idea of going in before they called Harper, but he'd put off the inevitable for a full fifteen minutes. If he didn't agree to going in soon, Amber would likely ignore him and go in anyway. Keeping her reasonably cooperative was essential.

"As soon as that customer comes out," he promised, "we're going in."

Amber acquiesced to his latest delay tactic with nothing more than a roll of her eyes.

The shop was in a small building on Pearson Avenue. Thrasher was thirty-one, the same age as Kyle Adler. Birmingham and its surrounding suburbs made for a fairly large population, so the two might not have grown up in the same neighborhood or have gone to school together, but they knew each other. Adler made deliveries for the floral shop—two of those deliveries had carried cards with warnings. Sean was damned certain a third one had, as well; he just couldn't prove it.

Since Adler was dead, who had delivered Amber's flowers? Thrasher? He'd denied making the delivery and claimed the employee who filled the order was out sick when Harper questioned him. If Harper had located the employee and questioned her, Sean hadn't heard about it. There was a lot happening in a short period of time. So much so that keeping everyone in the loop was difficult. Not that he and Amber had been keeping anyone informed. That had to change soon. They were way over the line already. Jess wouldn't be happy. The boss considered B&C's relationship with the BPD sacred. Maybe he'd still have a job when this case was finished.

At this point, he didn't have much to lose by putting off calling Harper for a few more minutes. If they were going to do this, they might as well do it right. It was time to ask Thrasher different questions.

The entrance opened, and the brunette they'd

been watching at the counter exited with a small arrangement.

"That's our cue." He climbed from behind the wheel and moved around to meet Amber on the sidewalk. "Careful what you say," he warned. "We need him cooperative, not defensive."

She made a face. "Trust me—I've done this once or twice, Mr. Douglas."

"So I'm Mr. Douglas now?"

She eyed him skeptically. "For the moment."

Shaking his head, he opened the door. The bell jingled as they entered. The lady behind the counter looked up. "Good afternoon. Welcome to Thrasher's. How can I help you?"

"Is Mr. Thrasher in?" Amber asked, taking the lead.

Sean suppressed a grin. She might be petite, but there was nothing small about her personality. She was pretty damned fearless. Like most people who met her in person for the first time, he'd thought she would be taller, too. He decided then and there the reason was her personality. Amber Roberts was larger than life.

The clerk shook her head. "He called me this morning and said he was sick. I rushed over and opened the shop."

"Thank you—" Sean noted the name on

her badge "—Louanne. We'll try to catch him again later."

Amber glared at him as he guided her out the same door they had just entered.

"What're you doing? I want to have a look around in that shop."

He ushered her to the car and opened her door. "Get in and I'll explain."

With a reluctant huff, she dropped into the seat. Sean hurried around to the driver's side and joined her.

"Let's go to his house." She dug through her purse. "I can locate his address in about thirty seconds."

"We have to call Harper. Now. No more putting it off." He pulled his cell from his pocket, ignoring her irritated glare. "We want whatever evidence we find to be admissible in court, Amber. We can't just go rummaging through the man's shop looking for clues."

"You didn't mention having issues with the idea when we were going through Rhiana's and Kimberly's homes."

"We had permission," he reminded her. "Their mothers were right there with us. We've gone as far as we can with this. It's time to let the cops do their job."

She stared at the street for a long moment. "Fine. Make the call."

Sean entered Harper's number and brought him up to speed. With the order to back off ringing in his ears, he ended the call and gave Amber the bad news.

"Detective Harper says it will take some time to get a warrant. He *suggested* we go home and wait for his call. The techs are finished at your place. He thinks it's safe if you want to go home."

"I knew this would happen." She folded her arms across her chest. "We should have nosed around when we had the chance."

He didn't bother pointing out once more that rendering evidence unusable was not their goal. "We skipped lunch. After what you went through last night, we need to rectify that oversight."

"I'm not hungry. I..."

When she remained silent, he glanced her way. She stared forward, her lips slightly parted. He licked his own and shifted his attention back to the street. The woman had amazing lips. He'd spent a lot of time watching those lips, and even when she'd been sick as a dog in the wee hours of the morning they were still tempting.

"We've been so focused on finding the evidence," she said, more to herself than to him. "We've ignored what it means." She turned to him. Her eyes round with something like disbelief. "They were watching us, and I don't mean from afar. I'm talking about up close."

Sean braked for a four-way stop. "Adler and Thrasher?"

She nodded, her gaze seeking his. "The flowers were delivered the day before each victim went missing. Mine had been ordered several days before they were delivered. They were watching." She pressed a hand to her lips. "One or the other or maybe both came into my house—into their houses—and took souvenirs, but that's not all they did while they were there."

A horn blared behind them, forcing Sean to take his eyes off her and to move forward. He got where she was headed. "You're thinking they planted cameras so they could watch."

"Oh, my God." Both hands went to her face then. "There's no other explanation."

Harper hadn't mentioned finding any surveillance devices. Sean reached over and took her hand in his. "You're okay. Adler is dead, and we're on to Thrasher. Whatever one or both did, it won't happen again."

She scrubbed at her eyes. "We have to search my house. Now. I need to know if they were watching me… I need to be sure."

"Since no other toxins have been found, I think it's safe to have a look. But I'm not letting you stay there again until this is over." Sean gave her hand a squeeze before letting go.

She held his gaze a beat longer. "Okay."

His entire being aching to lean across the seat and kiss her. He shifted his attention straight ahead. What he really wanted to do was pull over and make her feel this raging desire building inside him. She needed kissing. She needed to feel safe and cared for. For the first time in a very long time, he hoped he got the opportunity to make her feel that way.

Forest Brook Drive, Homewood

AMBER STARED AT her home for a long moment after the car stopped moving. Sean was getting out and would be at her door any second, but she suddenly couldn't move. Growing up, she had spent endless hours in this house. Louisa Roberts had been the perfect grandmother. She always baked cookies for Amber's arrival. If it was summer, there would be fresh-squeezed lemonade. If it was winter, there would be homemade hot chocolate. They read together and played games. Grandma Louisa owned every good board game made between 1950 and 1980, she'd boasted.

In this house Amber had felt completely safe and loved her entire life.

Until now.

Her door opened, and Sean waited for her to climb out. She stared up at him, conscious of her need to throw herself into his arms. She suddenly felt so isolated and completely alone. He was the one person that made her feel remotely safe right now. She wanted to know the shelter of his arms…she wanted to know him.

Shaking off the overwhelming reactions, she emerged from the car and steadied herself. When this was over, she intended to take a serious vacation. She hadn't taken a real vacation since the summer she graduated college. The job at the station was already hers, so she'd taken two weeks on the West Coast to relax and shop for a fashionable wardrobe. She'd returned well rested and seriously broke. Her grandmother had laughed and given her a high five. That winter Louisa Roberts had passed away.

Amber pushed aside the tender memories

and waited while Sean unlocked her front door. The silence inside made her belly clench. Normally her security system would be screaming for attention, but she had left it disarmed for the police. Actually, they hadn't armed it when they'd raced out of here headed for the ER. How had this place that had once felt so safe suddenly become so filled with potential danger?

Her heart was pounding by the time she crossed the threshold. As terrifying as the reality that someone had broken in and touched her things was, it was still good to be home on a level no one could touch.

The evidence technicians hadn't left the mess she had expected. Everything looked just as she'd left it when they'd hurried off to the ER last night. The teacup she'd used as well as the can of tea were missing. Both were evidence now. In a day or two the lab would be able to tell her what sort of poison had been added to her tea. She'd done some Google searches before she'd fallen asleep this morning, but the symptoms for most toxins were so similar it was impossible to narrow down the possibilities. She was, however, relatively certain the culprit was some sort of plant.

"Where should we begin?" she asked, shifting to what they'd come here to do.

"The cameras might be really small. Basically they could be planted anywhere, but—" he met her gaze "—we should check the bedroom and bathroom first."

The idea made Amber sick to her stomach. "How do you want to do this?"

"Do you have a stepladder?"

She nodded. "In the garage."

Rather than go to her bedroom, Amber waited in the living room for Sean to return. She hoped the feeling of uncertainty in her own home would pass quickly. When this was over and she was on that nice, long vacation, she intended to have the house cleaned and painted. All the food products were going in the trash. Every dish and spoon and utensil would be sanitized in the dishwasher. Every single item she owned was going to be washed or dry-cleaned.

It was the only way she would ever feel comfortable in her home again.

While Sean checked the overhead light fixtures and tops of the windows, Amber started the challenging task of going through the bookshelves and clutter on the chest of drawers and dresser.

"Here we go."

She turned from the bookshelf to see him take a small object from the narrow shelf made by the plantation shutters on the window. Her heart lurched.

"We need a box," he said. "A shoe box, hatbox, whatever you have handy."

Amber rushed into her closet and grabbed the first shoe box she could get her hands on. She dumped the contents and hurried back to where he waited. He placed the small gadget in the box. She positioned the lid over it. If the thing was still live, she didn't want whoever might be watching to see anything else.

Before moving on to the next room, they covered every square foot of her bedroom and discovered one more camera, this one on top of a family portrait that her grandmother had commissioned when Amber's father was five. Even if the evidence techs had moved the painting, they wouldn't have noticed it unless they were looking specifically for something so tiny.

A third camera was found in the bathroom on the cabinet above the toilet, angled to ensure she was captured taking a bath or shower. The fear she had felt earlier was gone. Fury had taken its place. This was her home! The living room and the kitchen were bugged with one camera each. She stood in the middle of her kitchen now and allowed the rage to course through her. It was either that or throw up, and she'd done enough of that last night.

"We should take all this to Harper," Sean suggested.

Amber didn't argue.

When they left she armed the security system for all the good it would do.

Sean called Lieutenant Harper, who suggested they meet at Thrasher's home since he was en route there with a warrant.

"Did they find him?" Amber wanted to know. Sean hadn't mentioned the floral shop owner.

He shook his head. "One of the neighbors said he left this morning at the same time he always does to open the shop and he hasn't returned."

"He's gone." Amber didn't need confirmation. The man knew the police were getting close to figuring out his connection to Adler and the murdered women and he'd run. *Damn it!*

"I'm sure the BPD issued a BOLO. Thrasher won't get far."

Amber hoped he was right.

Killough Circle, 6:15 p.m.

A BPD CRUISER sat on the street in front of the house belonging to Peter Thrasher. The sedan Lieutenant Chet Harper and Detective Chad Cook had arrived in was parked in the driveway alongside the evidence techs' van. Yellow tape marked the area as a crime scene. The two uniforms guarding the perimeter had informed Amber and Sean they had to wait on the street until further notice. Two other cruisers had blocked both ends of the block. No reporters were getting in.

Amber had been pacing the sidewalk for a good forty-five minutes. She was dying to know what was going on inside the house. Had they found evidence tying Thrasher to Adler? She rubbed at her forehead. Had they found photos or videos of her or the other women?

She hugged her arms around herself and paced in the other direction. Had the two sold the intimate look at her life to some adult site? Her stomach churned. If they had uploaded the videos they made to the internet…

"You're going to wear out that sidewalk," Sean commented.

Amber stalled and glared at him. Leaning against his car, his arms folded across his chest, ankles crossed, he appeared completely unperturbed. How could he look so calm? Two women had been murdered. She would have been number three if someone hadn't killed Adler. She might still end up murdered if Thrasher wasn't found. Reality washed over her like a dash of icy water. She would be looking over her shoulder for the rest of her life if he got away.

She couldn't fall apart now. *Deep breath.* "We've been waiting almost an hour." She looked back at the house. "Do you think they've found evidence to connect him to the cameras we found in my house?" She had stood outside the yellow tape at plenty of scenes where a crime had been committed. In her experience the longer the investigators were inside, the more likely the findings were significant.

"Chances are if they'd found nothing, we'd know it by now."

Of course they had found evidence. She really was out of sorts here. How long had she been reporting the news? Going on seven years. Granted, she rarely landed the major crime stories like serial killer Eric Spears—that was Gina Coleman's domain. Frankly, it didn't matter how many times she had worked a crime scene like this; this was different. This was personal. She was on the other side of the event this time. The reporters following this case were talking about her, which was in part why her boss had insisted she take a few vacation days. She'd been thinking about calling to do exactly that. He'd beat her to it.

Sean abruptly straightened away from his car. Amber's gaze followed his to the detective exiting the front door of Thrasher's home. Her pulse fluttered.

Detective Cook was only a couple of years younger than Amber. She'd seen him at Gina and Barb's engagement party. Cook had just popped the question to Dr. Sylvia Baron's daughter. Amber remembered feeling vaguely jealous of the couple. They had looked so in love.

Her gaze drifted to Sean. She blinked and looked away. God help her.

Cook gave Sean one of those male nods of acknowledgment, then he turned to Amber. "Ma'am, Lieutenant Harper will be out shortly. He'll brief you on what we found."

"Thank you." It was about time.

"We've got Ricky Vernon headed over here to take a look at the computers," Cook said to Sean. "Harper doesn't want to risk triggering any safety features that might shut down or wipe the systems."

"Are you saying there's more than one computer?" Amber's stomach sank.

Cook shifted his attention back to her. She held her breath as he seemed to decide how much he could tell her. "Yes, ma'am, four desktop computers and one laptop. It looks like he was watching a fourth woman. The lieutenant has sent a couple of uniforms over to check on her."

"Is she okay?"

Cook hesitated again. "We're not seeing her on any of the cameras. We've made a couple of calls already, and she wasn't at work today."

"Thrasher may have taken her." A chill bored into Amber's bones. And he was out there somewhere. She turned all the way around, scanning the neighborhood. He could be anywhere.

Chapter Twelve

Magic City Beer & Burger, 8:00 p.m.

Amber needed to relax. She sat on her side of the booth, her back ramrod straight. Sean had hoped that coming to an out-of-the-way place—one he doubted she'd ever set foot inside—would help make that happen. No such luck. She jumped every time the bell over the door jingled with a new customer.

"You should stop worrying about who walks in and just eat." He nodded to the house special on her plate. "You know the sauce is a closely guarded secret."

"I'm sure it's great." She forced a smile into place. "I'm really not hungry."

"The fries are the best in town." For emphasis he stuffed one into his mouth. Bad move. Rather than follow his example, she watched him chew. Out in LA he'd dated plenty of celebrity types. Every single one had been unique, but the one thing they all had in common was the inability to hide certain basic feelings. The flare of desire he spotted in Amber's green eyes startled him almost as much as he felt certain it did her. They'd had a couple of moments the past few days, but this was the first time she'd shown true hunger, and he was relatively certain it wasn't about the food.

"Eat," he encouraged. "You'll thank me later. Besides, you don't want to offend the chef."

She glanced over at the counter as the owner and cook shouted, "Order up," and placed a meatloaf special on the counter of the pass through window. With a sigh, she picked up her burger and took a bird-size bite. The surprise that captured her expression made him smile.

"I told you." He tore off another bite of his own sandwich.

For a few minutes they ate in silence. Amber stopped sizing up every customer who entered, and she ate not only the burger but every single fry. Apparently the lady hadn't realized how much she liked burgers. She'd polished off a good-size one at the Garage Café, too. All this time he'd been watching her on the news he'd had her figured for a vegan.

She patted her lips with her napkin. "Wow. I can't believe I ate so much."

"Good." He tossed his own crumpled napkin into his now-empty serving dish. "Would you like dessert? They make the best deep-fried Oreo cookie on the planet."

Amber held up her hands. "No, thanks. I couldn't eat another bite."

"Coffee then," he suggested.

She nodded. "Coffee would be great."

Sean waved over the waitress and ordered coffee. When she was on her way, he watched as Amber drifted back into her own troubling thoughts. "They'll find him."

She blinked as if resurfacing from a faraway place. "I hope so."

"Harper and Cook are the best."

She nodded. "They were part of the team Jess had when she was still with the department."

Sean's boss was pretty much a celebrity herself. "Lori Wells and Clint Hayes were on the team, too." Clint was the senior investigator at B&C now. One of the things Sean liked most about the older man was his straightforwardness. He didn't tolerate the games some people liked to play. Amber appeared to share that feeling. So far Sean had found her to be honest and direct. He liked that about her.

"Gina is always telling stories about Jess's FBI days and how her profiles were responsible for bringing down the worst of the worst."

"Eric Spears." Sean was still living in Hollywood when the infamous serial killer followed Jess to Birmingham, but he'd heard plenty about it from his family.

"Eric Spears was at the top of the evil scale," Amber said. "Gina did an exposé on the way Jess profiled using a scale she called the faces of evil." She laughed. "I'm sure you've heard a great deal about how amazing your boss is."

"She is amazing and tough." Sean had experienced the latter firsthand.

Amber pushed her empty plate aside and braced her crossed arms on the table. She leaned forward and looked directly into his eyes. "How many other women have been hurt or murdered by Thrasher and Adler? What if Pettie and McCorkle weren't their first victims?"

"Jess doesn't think there were other victims, but we may never know for sure," Sean allowed. The waitress arrived with two steaming cups of coffee. Sean gifted her with a smile and thanked her. He sipped his coffee, hoping Amber would do the same rather than dwell on the what-ifs.

When she followed his lead and tasted the coffee, she made an approving sound. "This place is full of surprises."

The place looked a little rough on the surface, especially with the old truck front end hanging on the wall behind the bar. Rustic but homey in Sean's opinion. The staff was extra friendly, and the craft beers were second to none. "My folks used to bring us here here as kids. It was a ritual after church on Sundays."

Amber smiled, that genuine one that made his heart beat a little faster. "You went to church?"

"Didn't you?" he teased. "You grew up in Birmingham—you must have."

"I did. I still do occasionally. Work sometimes gets in the way." She sipped her coffee and turned thoughtful for a moment. "Even when we traveled, we found a house of worship. Whether it was a Jewish temple or a Buddhist one. My parents embrace all people and their cultures."

"More people should raise their children that way." Sean damned sure intended to—if he ever had any. Now there was a thought that came out of left field. Just because he would turn thirty this year didn't mean time was running out. As far as he knew guys didn't have so-called biological clocks. He drowned the crazy idea with more coffee.

"Why does Jess believe there aren't other murder victims?" Amber's smile had disappeared. The worry was back in her eyes.

"She read the case files on Pettie and McCorkle. She concluded that the first murder, Pettie, was likely a surprise to both men. The work was sloppier. They were more careful and organized with the second victim, McCorkle. Even the way the cameras were placed in the homes, Pettie's versus yours, was progressively more precise."

"So they may have started out as Peeping Toms hiding in the girls' bathroom at school or watching their sisters or mothers?"

"Exactly. The BPD confirmed the two attended the same schools. Jess believes they probably teamed up as school chums and things grew from there."

Amber shivered visibly. Sean reached across the table and placed his hand on hers. "Even if Thrasher is stupid enough to try, he'll have to go through me to get to you."

A faint smile trembled across her lips. "I'm really grateful you're here."

The warmth that had spread up his arm and across his chest from nothing more than touching her hand had him wondering how grateful she would be if she knew how much he wanted to touch all of her.

She straightened away from the table, breaking the contact. "I think maybe I'll have one of those deep-fried Oreos after all."

Rather than summon the waitress, Sean went to the counter and placed the order. He needed the distance. Allowing personal involvement with a client was a mistake he did not intend to repeat. Too bad the only part of him sticking by that motto was his brain—everything else was pulsing with need. He returned to the booth only a few minutes later with their desserts, and they both dug in.

Whether the sugar rush had her thinking again or just gave her the courage to do so, she waded into sensitive territory. "Do you think they shared the videos on the internet? Will the FBI have to be involved?"

"The guy from the BPD's lab is the top in his field. He'll be able to determine how far the sharing went, if at all," Sean explained. "If Adler and Thrasher were sharing their peep shows with friends via the Net, the FBI will more than likely be involved."

She shuddered. "I feel so exposed."

He understood. It was one thing for her to report the news on camera, but another one entirely for her private moments bathing and dressing to be videoed without her knowledge or consent. He knew a little something about feeling exposed.

"We'll know more about what we're looking at tomorrow," he promised.

"I hope they find the other woman alive." She nibbled at another bite of her dessert. "The timing would be right, you know, for another kidnapping. Pettie was in February, McCorkle in June. October makes four months. Isn't that the way serial killers work?"

"Most have a pattern." He nodded. "If Thrasher stuck to the pattern he and Adler followed and abducted a fourth victim, he did so in the past twenty-four hours. Since the other vics were held for several days before they were murdered, it makes sense that she would still be alive. Assuming, of course, the death of his partner hasn't sent him off in a different direction."

Amber sat her coffee down and stared into the cup for a moment as if searching for the right words. "Why do you suppose I was skipped? It was obvious they'd been watching me longer."

"If Thrasher murdered Adler, we have to assume the two had a falling-out. I imagine the event put Thrasher into a tailspin. Before he could regain his bearings the body was discovered and you were brought in for questioning. I've been with you since. My guess is he moved on to the next name on the list."

Amber leaned her head in her hand and rubbed her temple with her fingers. "I guess I'm the lucky one."

Sean had learned enough from Jess to know luck had nothing to do with it. Something went down between Thrasher and Adler that disrupted the timeline of the two killers. In Sean's opinion it was somehow related to Amber.

He wished the feeling that it was far from over would stop gnawing at him.

Oxmoor Glen Drive, 9:15 p.m.

SEAN TOSSED THE tennis ball across the room, and the big dog bounced after it. When he tried to take the ball back a tug-of-war ensued. Amber moistened her lips and bit back a grin. She found it far too endearing that her bodyguard played with his dog as if it were a child. He obviously loved the animal. She'd never had time for pets. Come to think of it, she rarely found time for anything other than work. Why was it the idea suddenly felt so wrong?

When Rebel had tired of playing, he curled up on the fluffy round bed in the corner. Sean gestured to the sofa. "Feel free to turn on the television. I should make sure the guest room is presentable."

"I slept in it for a couple of hours this morning," she reminded him. "I didn't have any complaints. Besides, why would I turn on the television and listen to all the speculation and theories connecting me to Adler's murder?"

"Good point." He backed into the hallway and then disappeared.

Amber released a long, weary breath and surveyed Sean's place. She hadn't really taken in many of the details in the wee hours of this morning. The kitchen, dining and living space were one fairly large room. The place was nice with most modern amenities. A gas fireplace in the living room, stainless steel appliances in the kitchen and nice high ceilings. The decor was American bachelor simple: big, comfy sofa, huge television hanging over the fireplace and a coffee table littered with sports magazines and remotes.

On the bar that separated the kitchen from the rest of the space where he'd tossed his keys, there was a framed photograph of a young Sean, his siblings and their parents. His hair was considerably longer. She estimated the shot had been taken before he left for the West Coast. A built-in bookcase next to the fireplace held several books by one of her favorite mystery authors. She reached for last year's release and smiled. So they had something besides the lack of a personal life in common after all.

"Have you picked up his latest?"

Amber closed the book and tucked it back onto the shelf. "I haven't, but I plan to. You?"

"It's on my bedside table. You're welcome to it."

Was he inviting her to his bed or to borrow his book? Her nerves jangled foolishly. She was nervous. The realization startled her. Hoping to keep that embarrassing revelation to herself, she pointed at him and gave a knowing nod. "You saw the stack on my bedside table, didn't you?"

He shrugged. "I might have noticed." He glanced at the clock in the cable box. "Would you like a beer?" Another of those completely male shrugs lifted his shoulders. "Sorry. I've been meaning to pick up a good bottle of wine for company. I'm pretty sure I have popcorn and a stash of peanuts."

Was it her imagination or was he feeling as nervous as she was? "Nothing for me, thank you."

For several seconds they stood there staring at each other.

She should say something. "I think I might shower and go to bed early." She propped her lips into a broad smile. "Do a little reading maybe—if you don't mind me borrowing that book."

"Sure thing." He hitched a thumb over his shoulder. "I'll get it for you."

Scrubbing her unexpectedly sweaty palms against her hips, she followed him down the short hall. Butterflies had taken flight in her belly. She stopped at the door rather than follow him into his bedroom. Like the main living space, the decorating was minimal. A big bed, bedside table and a chest of drawers. She was surprised not to see another massive television. What she did see was a stack of books that rivaled her own.

He grabbed a pair of boxers and a lone shoe

from the floor. "You need anything else to sleep in?"

She thought of the faded crimson tee that sported the Roll Tide logo she'd slept in that morning. "The T-shirt works."

"There're clean towels in the bathroom closet." He winced. "Did your sister bring bodywash? You might not like my soap. I know you used it this morning, but that was kind of an emergency."

"It's fine." It smelled like him, but she'd been too sick to care.

He tossed the shoe and boxers into his closet and then grabbed the hardcover from the bedside table. He crossed the room, coming toward her, and her heart beat considerably faster. She tried to swallow, but her throat felt closed.

He passed the book to her. "If you get past the sixth chapter, don't tell me if he gets the girl."

Her fingers brushed his and need ignited deep inside her. "Doesn't he always get the girl?"

Sean was so close now the scent of his skin filled her senses. She wanted to reach out and run her hands over those broad shoulders. She wanted to trace every ridge and valley of the lean torso beneath that khaki shirt. She wanted to lose herself in the sensations and pretend her world wasn't a total mess.

He leaned his face toward hers. "I would really like to kiss you right now, but that's a bad idea."

She lifted her face, leaving no more than a couple of inches between their lips. "I was thinking the same thing."

He moistened his lips, and her breath caught.

"What do you want to do about it?"

Amber reached up slowly and fisted her fingers in his shirt. "I say we get it over with so we can move past it." She wet her lips. "My grandmother always said to go for whatever you wanted, otherwise you'd just go on wanting it."

"Smart lady."

His lips lowered to hers. The first contact had pure pleasure erupting inside her. His mouth was hot, his lips firm, but his kiss was slow and restrained. His fingers landed on her cheeks, tracing the lines of her face as his lips tasted and teased hers. She pulled at his shirt, drawing that amazing body nearer.

By the time he drew his lips from hers, her thighs were trembling and every part of her was on fire. He pressed his forehead to hers and whispered, "That was good."

"Uh-huh." She licked her lips, shivering at the taste of him.

"Should we do it again just to make sure we get it out of our systems?"

Amber closed her eyes and inhaled a slow, deep breath. She wanted to say yes so badly. "I think we should maybe wait until tomorrow and revisit the idea then." Otherwise she was going to drag him into that big, unmade bed.

"Agreed."

He drew away first and stuffed his hands into the pockets of his jeans as if he didn't trust himself.

Amber's entire being protested the loss of contact. "Well, good night."

He managed a stiff nod. "'Night."

Amber didn't breathe again until she was in the guest room with the door closed. She tossed the book onto the bed and dragged in a couple more deep breaths to calm her galloping pulse. When she felt in control again, she grabbed the tee and some clean underwear. She opened the door and peeked into the hall. Clear. She moved to the bathroom. He'd gone back to the living room and turned on the television. Once inside the bathroom, she closed the door and locked it. A glance in the mirror made her wince. She looked frightful. Her skin was even paler than usual. Dark circles had formed under her eyes.

With a groan, she turned on the water in the shower and undressed. How in the world had she allowed that to happen? What had she been thinking? Shaking her head, she stepped into the shower, and the hot water instantly banished all other thought.

For a while she stood there and allowed the water to work its magic on her tight muscles. It felt so good. She'd been so tense all day. Slowly, she reached for the soap and lathered it up. The clean, fresh scent of Sean filled the tiled space. She shivered despite the hot water.

A glutton for punishment, she closed her eyes and rubbed the soap over her skin. When she moved it over her breasts, her breath caught and she let the memory of his kiss consume her. By the time she'd lathered her skin, her body felt weak with want. In her mind his hands replaced hers, sliding the soap over her skin, his fingers tempting her nipples and trailing down her ribs. She trembled.

The soap slipped from her fingers and hit the floor. Amber jerked out of the fantasy. This was a perfect example of how badly the past few days had shaken her. She was fantasizing about a stranger. Sure they had spent the last forty-eight or so hours together, but they still didn't know each other.

Hurrying through the rest of her shower, she rinsed her body with cool water. Even after she'd toweled off, she was still burning up. She dragged on the tee and her underwear and reached for the door. Maybe she should give herself a few more minutes before chancing an encounter with Sean.

After taking a deep breath, she prowled for a hair dryer and set to the task. She massaged her scalp with one hand while directing the hot air with the other. Her fingers slowed as she studied her reflection. What did Sean Douglas see when he looked at her? She was attractive enough, she supposed. Braces had taken care of her teeth back in middle school. She hadn't suffered with acne like a lot of her friends, but she'd been teased endlessly about her freckles.

She didn't mind the freckles really. The makeup when she was on the air basically covered them up, but she didn't bother trying to hide them when she wasn't on the job. She hung her towel over the shower door while the dryer cooled off, and then she searched the cabinet under the sink for a spare toothbrush. She'd left hers in the guest room.

A knock at the door made her jump. She bumped her head on the counter.

"I noticed your toothbrush on the bedside table," Sean announced, his deep voice filtering through the door and wrapping around her. "You want it?"

Man alive did she want it, only it wasn't the toothbrush. Amber rubbed at her head. She cracked the door open the tiniest bit and reached out. "Thanks."

He placed the toothbrush in her waiting hand. "Welcome."

When he walked away she closed the door and leaned against it for a long moment. *Get a grip, Amber. Adrenaline is messing with your head.*

Five minutes later, teeth brushed, dryer put away and her clothes folded in her arms, she exited the bathroom and headed straight for the guest room. "See you in the morning," she called without a backward glance.

His deep voice followed her into the room. "Count on it."

Chapter Thirteen

Fourth Avenue North,
Thursday, October 20, 10:20 a.m.

The story was out.

For six years Amber had chased the story. She had gone to great lengths to uncover details and insights no one else could find.

Now *she* was the story.

She and Sean had been summoned to the B&C office right after breakfast. On some level she was glad for the escape. All night the memory of that kiss had haunted her. Meeting his gaze this morning had been difficult. Primarily because she'd wanted to resume right where they'd left off. *So, so not smart.*

On the way here, she'd focused on the case, hoping the summons meant there was good news, but judging by the look on Jess Burnett's face that was not the case. Buddy Corlew had called first thing this morning to let them know the phone records had been a bust. There were plenty of calls between Adler and his customers, but none between him and Thrasher except those to the floral shop.

Amber braced for more bad news.

Jess closed the folder on her desk and looked first at Amber, then at Sean. "Thrasher is still at large. His car was found abandoned near the Nineteenth Street bus station. It's possible he fled the city, but there's always the chance he could be in hiding close by."

It wasn't necessary to be an FBI profiler to understand why Thrasher would choose not to run. "He may want to finish what he and Adler started," Amber proposed.

Jess nodded. "Lieutenant Harper and I believe it would be best if you continued to keep a low profile for a few more days. We want to be sure you stay safe."

"Wow." Amber slumped in her chair. "This keeps growing more complicated." So many times she had interviewed victims and expressed her sympathy. Now she understood the look in their eyes after she offered the usual words of commiseration. A person couldn't possibly understand how *this* felt…unless he or she was the target. "So *you* believe I'm still in danger."

"I do. I've had time to review all the available information on Thrasher and Adler," Jess began. "Thrasher has spent his adult life dealing in flowers. He never married. No long-term relationships. His father died when he was ten and his mother passed away two years ago, so there's no family. No record of mental illness or counseling of any sort. No health issues on record. According to the interviews conducted by the lieutenant's team, his employees like him."

"Is that typical in a killer?" Sean asked.

The sound of his voice wrapped around Amber and made breathing difficult. She wasn't at all sure she could handle another night in the same house with him. She'd gone to sleep and awakened dreaming of making love with him. His voice, the way he moved, it all got under her skin somehow.

"Many killers are loners," Jess explained. "Most psychopaths are quite charming. Not all are murderers. In fact, I'm not convinced Thrasher is a killer. Adler may have been the dominant one, but I haven't found evidence suggesting as much. According to the interviews conducted by the BPD, Adler's parents are very religious. They raised their son in a strict environment. Those who knew him called him a loner, shy, quiet. Nothing was found in either man's home that tells us the rest of what we need to know." Jess clasped her hands atop the folder. "I'm not willing to take the risk there's another layer to one or both that I'm not seeing yet. Until we know more, we need to make sure you stay safe."

Sean glanced at Amber. "I guess that means you're stuck with me for a little while longer."

She produced a smile. "I guess so."

"If Thrasher and Adler were obsessed with you," Jess said, "he won't be able to stay away. He'll need to see you. To be close."

Her words sent goose bumps spilling over Amber's skin. "I understand. The station isn't expecting me back to work for a few days." She swallowed, wishing her mouth hadn't gone so dry. "I should stay home and not answer the door?"

A rap on the door drew Jess's attention there. Amber glanced over her shoulder to see the receptionist poke her head into the office.

"There are at least a dozen reporters lining

the street out front. When Ms. Roberts is ready to leave I would suggest the alley exit."

Any hope of getting through this without mounting attention in the media curled up and died in the pit of Amber's stomach.

"Thank you, Rebecca." Jess shifted her attention to Amber. "The more your face is in the news, the more Thrasher will be incited to make a move—if he's watching, as I suspect he is. If he's obsessed with you, he can't help himself."

"How difficult do you believe it'll be for the police to find him?" Amber pressed.

"His resources are limited, which helps, but there's no guarantee he'll be found."

She could be looking over her shoulder for the rest of her life. This time the inability to draw in a deep breath had nothing to do with the man next to her. Something Jess had said suddenly elbowed its way to the front of her worries. "You said you're not convinced Thrasher is a killer and that there's no absolute evidence Adler is. If they aren't killers, then who murdered those women?"

"Therein lies the rub," Jess admitted. "Consider Adler's murder. He was seated at the dining table having tea, presumably with his killer. If that killer was Thrasher, who is a far larger man than Adler, why get up from the table and go to the kitchen for a knife when you can easily overtake the victim?"

"You think there's a third killer involved." It wasn't a question. Amber could see the conviction in Jess's eyes.

"Lieutenant Harper has expanded the parameters of his investigation to include a potential third killer," Jess explained. "In my opinion, it's a necessary step."

Amber felt completely unnerved. Totally unsettled. "Wow."

"I would advise you to go someplace not a part of your routine," Jess offered. "Someplace the killer or killers won't know to look. Just for a few days. Let the BPD and us do what we need to do without having to worry about adding names to the victim list."

"What about the other woman who was being watched?" Amber worried Jess hadn't provided an update on the woman because it was more bad news. "Has she been found?"

"She has," Jess said. "Her name is Emma Norton. The employee the BPD spoke to had just returned from vacation and didn't realize Emma had taken her vacation this week. The lieutenant has spoken to her. She's visiting her father in Seattle. I received the call just before you arrived."

"I'm glad to hear it." Amber felt immensely relieved. It was bad enough two women were dead.

"Take a day or two someplace quiet while we sort this out," Jess repeated. "Sean will see that you stay safe."

He stood. "I'll make sure the alley is still clear."

Amber pushed to her feet. "I appreciate all you're doing, Jess. I can't imagine doing this alone."

With effort Jess stood and rested a hand on her rounded belly. "I'm glad we can help. You are our top priority."

Sean returned and ushered Amber to the rear entrance. Since the slots in front of the B&C office had been full when they arrived, he'd parked two blocks away. To avoid being spotted by her colleagues from the various stations around the city, they detoured another couple of blocks.

He opened her door, and Amber settled in the passenger seat. What if Thrasher wasn't found by Monday? How long was she supposed to keep her life on hold? She should call Barb and let her know what was going on. Was her sister in danger? Jess hadn't mentioned any concerns about Barb's safety. Calling her boss was unavoidable. He would insist she take as much time as she needed.

She didn't want to take more time. She wanted her life back. She wanted to avoid getting tangled up with her protector. She wanted to stay alive.

Amber looked around to get her bearings. She couldn't say how long Sean had been driving before she snapped out of her pity party. "Where are we going?"

"My parents have a place on the river. I thought we'd go there."

She hoped it was larger than his house. "What about clothes?" And other stuff, like a toothbrush and deodorant?

"We can drive past your house, but I'm guessing there are more reporters waiting there. We can stop for what we need once we're out of the city."

Amber resigned herself to her fate. It was either risk a confrontation with an obsessed killer or killers or spend time in a remote location alone with the man who had kissed her like she'd never before been kissed.

She stole a glance at him. She was in trouble either way.

River Road, 3:30 p.m.

JUST OVER A year ago Sean had escaped the hurt and anger by coming here. For six months after Lacy's death the press hounded him. The official investigation had cleared him of any criminal wrongdoing related to her death, but he hadn't been able to forgive himself. If he had paid closer attention…if he hadn't allowed things to become personal, she might still be alive.

Intellectually he understood that the choices she had made in her life were not his responsibility, but in his heart he carried the burden. He had trusted her…trusted the love they shared.

What an arrogant fool he'd been.

"So this is where your family spends Christmas?"

Sean shook off the painful memories and focused on the woman standing in the middle of the family room. "This is the place."

During the forty-five-minute drive from the city she'd initially remained silent. He imagined she grappled for some way to come to terms with the situation. As if she'd reached some understanding with herself, she had kept the conversation going from that point on, asking him question after question about the family cabin. His great-great-grandfather had built the room they were now standing in nearly a hundred years ago. Each generation had added additional square footage and renovated to include multiple bedrooms and bathrooms. His grandmother had been the one to insist on the huge eat-in kitchen.

"Take any bedroom you'd like." The sooner they were settled, the sooner he could walk the grounds to clear his head. In the past twenty-four hours the lady had managed to breach his defenses entirely. That kiss had blown him away. Even a month ago he wouldn't have believed he could feel that way again. He wanted to touch her and to kiss her…and a whole lot more.

She's an assignment, blockhead. Work. You can't go there.

"Which one do you usually take?"

Her question dragged him from the disturbing thoughts just in time to watch her turn all the way around again, taking in the enormity of the place. There were no frills, no chef's kitchen or jetted tubs, just homey spaces with decent plumbing and incredible views of nature.

"Top of the stairs, first door on the left." He

hitched a thumb toward the door. "I'll batten down the hatches and bring in the supplies."

Since no one had stayed here since spring, there were a few things to be done before dark, like turning on the water and checking the generator in case there was a power outage. Then he had to bring in the food supplies and get the refrigerated goods stored. As long as he stayed busy, he would be good to go.

Maybe.

Sean did a quick walk-through of the house before heading outside. When he'd been a kid he'd dreamed of living here full-time. Of course puberty and girls had changed his mind. The occasional weekend here had felt like a world away from his school friends and whoever he'd been sweet on at the time. If only he had known how complicated life could be.

The sky was darker than usual. The rain would be here soon, along with a potential thunderstorm or two. All the more reason to check the generator. His father had taught him to ensure all the mechanics were in working order before getting comfortable. It wasn't like you could call for a service man who would show up in an hour or so.

With the water on and the generator checked, he took a walk around the house and confirmed all was as it should be. Down at the road a passing car drew his attention. He should probably call his parents and let them know he was here. Neighbors were few and far between out here, but they kept an eye on each other's property. His folks would no doubt get a call when the house lights were spotted tonight. Having his parents show up to investigate would not be a good thing. His mother had been complaining for years that she wanted grandchildren. Since his older siblings hadn't stepped up to the plate, his mother was now eyeing him to fill that void.

The image of little redheaded girls frolicking around the pond made his heart stumble. Shaking his head at the crazy fantasy, he carried the first load of grocery bags into the house. When he returned with the rest, Amber was putting away the refrigerated goods.

"You didn't tell me there was a basement with a wine cellar." She put the quart of milk in the fridge. "This is no run-of-the-mill cabin, sir."

"When my grandmother insisted on the kitchen expansion, my grandfather demanded the wine cellar with a smoking room."

A smile spread across her lips as she set the sandwich bread on the counter. Man, he loved the way she smiled. "Sounds like your grand-father knew how to drive a hard bargain."

"He did." Sean placed the bag of mixed greens in the fridge. "He died three years ago, barely three weeks after my grandmother."

"I'm so sorry."

He met her sympathetic gaze. "They were like that. Did everything together, and wher-ever one went, the other followed."

Sean had decided years ago his grandpar-ents had the kind of love that couldn't be found anymore. People had stopped learning how to love that way. For the most part his parents' re-lationship wasn't far off the mark. He couldn't hope to ever share that kind of devotion with anyone.

"My grandparents were like that." Amber scooted onto a stool at the kitchen's center island. "My parents, too. I never really no-ticed until they retired and started traveling so much. It's like they've fallen in love with each other all over again. My sister says she and Gina have that deep bond. I'm not so sure people our age know how to love like that. Maybe we can't give so deeply."

"Is that what you're looking for?" He could have bitten off his tongue. Why the hell had he asked that damned question? Because he was this close—he mentally imagined his thumb and forefinger a fraction of an inch apart—to being a fool twice in one lifetime. At least he hadn't announced that he'd just been thinking the same thing. He'd already noticed far too many commonalities between them.

Her brow furrowed as she contemplated the question. He busied himself with stuffing the plastic grocery bags into the recycle bin.

"I absolutely want it, just not now. My career is top priority." She drew in a big breath. "Before I'm forty I'd like to be married and focused on making a family."

He allowed his gaze to rest on hers once more. The seriousness in her green eyes made his gut tighten. "Sounds like a plan."

He could see himself taking a similar path when he was older. Just another example of how alike they thought. Sean stopped himself. He was intensely attracted to Amber and they had a great deal in common, but that didn't mean they belonged together. *Get your head out of your—*

"Would you mind taking a walk with me?"

Sean blinked. "Sorry. What?"

"I've felt like a prisoner for two days. I need to get outside, breathe some fresh air and just walk off some of the stress. I hate to ask, but apparently I'm not supposed to go anywhere alone."

"Sure." He reached for the key. Usually he wouldn't bother locking up for a stroll around the property, but this was different. Until Thrasher and whoever else might be involved were found, Amber had to be protected.

The sky had darkened a little more but there was still plenty of daylight for a short walk. Over the years several paths had been formed along interesting views on the property. A long circle around the pond and then a meandering trail through the woods to the river. The air was crisp but not actually cold.

Maybe a walk had been a good idea.

"Do you come here every Christmas?"

The soft, lyrical sound of her voice meshed perfectly with the natural beauty around them. Funny how he noticed all those little things when he didn't want to. He should never have kissed her. That sweet taste would never be enough. "I do."

"I'll bet you cut your Christmas tree from these very woods."

Sean laughed. "We do actually. My grandfather insisted that two be planted for each one we cut. Every year on Christmas Eve, my parents drag two small evergreens up here to plant."

"Your grandfather was a smart man."

Sean wished he were a lot smarter and maybe he wouldn't be standing here dying to kiss her again. Then again, maybe what he really needed was courage.

Chapter Fourteen

7:30 p.m.

The scent of marinara sauce filled the kitchen, and Amber's stomach grumbled. She placed the salad she'd prepared on the dining table. The long farmer's table seated ten. She could imagine the big family gatherings around the holidays. The large fireplace on the other side of the room would be roaring at Christmastime. The freshly cut tree would stand tall before the front window. She closed her eyes and imagined the smell of freshly baked cookies. Though her family holidays were usually celebrated in the city at her parents' Mountain Brook home, she'd gotten a taste of a true country Christmas as a child. Her grandparents on her mother's side had lived on a small farm in Blount County. She'd spent a few Christmases there.

She remembered the towering, freshly cut trees. Her grandparents always waited until Christmas Eve to place the final decoration on their tree. The star that topped its peak was saved for Amber's mother to set in place. Her grandmother insisted that her only child, Amber's mother, had placed that star atop the tree since she was old enough to hold it, and she wasn't letting go of that tradition as long as she was breathing.

By the time her grandmother reached thirty, she'd already been married with a daughter running around the home where she and her husband had started many wonderful traditions. Amber straightened the linen napkins next to the two plates. Her only traditions were spending holidays with her family—if work didn't get in the way. Those traditions were actually her parents', not hers. She didn't have any holiday traditions, or any other kind for that matter. She had work.

"Hot stuff headed your way," Sean announced as he moved around her to place the bowl of sauce and the mound of plated pasta on the table.

Amber bit her lips together to prevent mentioning that the food wasn't the only hot stuff in the room. Then and there she admitted defeat. The man got to her. He made her want to explore feelings she'd spent the past year telling herself she no longer cared about. After the breakup with her fiancé, she had decided she would wait a few years or ten before getting involved in another serious personal relationship. How had this man—in a mere seventy, give or take a few, hours—changed her mind so completely?

A hand waved in front of her face. "You still with me?"

Her gaze settled on his, and she melted a little more even as the sound of his deep voice made her shiver.

"Are you cold?" He rubbed his hands up and down her arms.

Her pulse skittered, and she mentally scrambled to find her voice. "No, no. I'm not cold at all." In fact, she was burning up.

"Sit." He pulled out a chair. "I'll run down to the cellar and get a bottle of wine."

Amber prepared her plate. A small serving of salad and pasta. The smell of the sauce had her mouth watering and her appetite resurrecting. Maybe eating was what she needed to take her mind off sex and Sean. Really, her inability to ignore her attraction to him surely had to do with twelve months of celibacy. Had she chosen to abstain from sex since the breakup? Not really. She simply hadn't taken the time to socialize.

The truth was she hadn't been on a date in six or seven months.

Sean returned with a bottle of wine and a bottle of water. He placed the bottle of water next to his glass and deftly opened the bottle of wine. He reached for her glass. "Say when."

Amber moistened her lips as he poured the red wine. "When," she remembered to say as the stemmed glass grew half full.

He set the bottle aside and claimed his chair. Rather than pour himself a glass of wine, he added water to his glass, and then reached for the pasta.

"You're not having wine?" She downed a hefty swallow to calm her nerves.

"Can't." He grinned as he smothered the angel-hair pasta with sauce.

The heat that had kindled inside her at just being in the same room with him extinguished. "Right. Of course. You're on duty." It was his job to be here with her.

She really, really was losing her grip. None of this was real. The silky texture of the full-bodied wine soured on her tongue. What was wrong with her? A man was dead, two innocent women—his victims—had been murdered. Being trapped on the radar of this former killing partnership had turned her life upside down. Had left her vulnerable to her own fundamental desires. The fear of death made her want to celebrate life. She downed another swallow of wine.

Since he'd already dug in, she forced herself to eat. Her appetite had vanished again, but she had the foresight to understand the wine would go straight to her head if she didn't eat. They had forgotten to pick up rolls. Saved her a few carbs.

"Is everything okay?"

She realized then that he'd already cleaned his plate and was going for seconds. "It's great." Another mouthful of wine covered the bitter taste of the lie.

He talked endlessly about his family and how much he'd missed the traditions when he'd lived in LA. To a large degree he felt the loving traditions of his family had helped him move past the tragedy. Amber hung on his every word—hard as she tried not to.

When he tossed his napkin aside, she realized he had stopped talking and was staring at her.

"Now I'm really worried."

She reached for her glass, but it was empty. She blinked and cleared her throat. "Worrying won't find the bad guy." She laughed. "We can do nothing but wait it out." The truth in her words made her shudder. There really was nothing she could do. For the first time in her adult life she felt helpless.

He reached out and entwined his fingers with hers. "This is hard—I know. We'll get to the bottom of what's going on soon. The BPD is moving quickly. Jess and Buddy are doing all they can." He squeezed her fingers. "I'm right here, and I'm not going anywhere until you're safe."

And then he would be gone.

Amber stood. "Thank you for a great meal. I'll be back to help clean up."

She hurried up the stairs to the room she'd chosen. She slammed the door shut and tried to calm her breathing. Squeezing her eyes shut, she cursed herself for jumping back into the pity pool. Her mood swings were about nothing more. She was a grown woman—an educated woman with a great career. There was no excuse for feeling sorry for herself. Yes, a bad man or men had put her life in danger, and, yes, her emotional neediness had prompted her to get all sentimental and filled with what-ifs, but this would be over eventually and she would be okay.

The least she could do was act like a grown-up about it instead of falling apart just because the man who had kissed her like she'd never been kissed before wasn't the knight in shin-ing armor with whom she was destined to ride off into the sunset.

And then she laughed. When the laughter started, she couldn't stop it. Two women were dead, and she was upset because her body-guard wasn't as enamored with her as she was with him.

A knock at the door had her wiping the tears from her eyes.

"You okay in there?"

Was she okay? *Absolutely not.* Would she be okay? *Probably.*

Squaring her shoulders and wiping her cheeks, she crossed to the door and opened it. "I'm perfectly fine."

He searched her face with those incredible blue eyes, and she realized that he really was worried about her state of mind.

Amber laughed. Startled at her reaction, she

pressed her fingers to her lips and muttered, "Sorry. I think I'm hysterical."

Concern lined his face. "Maybe I should get you another glass of wine."

Barely suppressing a second outburst of side-splitting laughter, she held up her hands stop-sign fashion. "No, no. Really, I'm fine. I just… I just…" She burst into tears. "Oh, God. I don't know what's wrong with me."

Could she do any more to embarrass herself? She simply could not get it together.

Sean pulled her into his strong arms and hugged her close. "Everything's going to be all right," he promised softly. "I'll keep you safe."

She drew away and shook her head. "I know the police will find Thrasher and whoever else is involved, and this will all be over eventually. That's not the reason I'm upset."

He squeezed her arm and smiled. "You're scared."

A burst of anger flared inside her, instantly drying the ridiculous tears. "I am not scared." She wasn't. She really wasn't. Not at the moment anyway. She had him…for protection.

He held up his hands in surrender. "Sorry. I'm only trying to help."

Calm down, Amber. It isn't his fault you're having trouble holding it together.

She smoothed a hand over her blouse and reclaimed her composure. "I apologize. I don't know why I fell apart there for a moment. I'm fine—I assure you. I should probably call it a night a little early."

Under no circumstances did she trust herself alone in the same room with him just now. She was on some sort of emotional roller coaster, and she had no idea where the tracks ran out. Ending up in bed with him was not where she wanted to crash-land tonight.

His face changed as if an epiphany had occurred to him. "Is this about that kiss last night?"

Her jaw dropped. The very idea that he would call it *that kiss* made her inexplicably angry. "What about the kiss? It happened in a moment of…a moment of neediness. It wasn't a big deal."

He frowned. "Ouch. I thought it was a huge deal." His gaze dropped to her lips. "I really hoped we might go for an encore." His gaze slid up to hers. "If you're as interested as it felt like you were."

A multitude of new sensations cascaded over her, shaking her newly regained composure. "I told you I don't do one-night stands." Even as she said the words she couldn't stop looking at his lips.

Before she could dodge the move, he had closed the short distance between them and forked his fingers into her hair. "Good, because I have no interest in a one-night stand with you." He pulled her mouth to his but hesitated before kissing her. "I want a whole lot more, starting with this."

He kissed her, his lips applying just the right amount of pressure. No matter that her mind was set to protest, her body melted against his. Her hands slid up his sculpted chest and curled around his neck. He cupped her bottom and lifted her into him, showing her the intensity of his desire.

"Say the word," he murmured against her lips, "and I'll stop."

"Don't stop." She kissed him hard, tangled her fingers in his hair and held his mouth firmly against hers.

He lifted her against him and carried her to the bed. They fell onto the plaid quilt together. He took his time undressing her and helping her nervous fingers undress him. It had been so long and she was so excited she couldn't seem to make her fingers work.

When they lay skin to skin, he slowed things

down even more. He kissed her gently, tracing her face with his fingertips. She did the same, loving the ridges and planes of his handsome face. The high cheekbones and square jaw, the straight nose and strong brow. The silky feel of his blond hair and the amazing blue of his eyes.

He whispered sweet words to her as he kissed his way down her throat. *You're so beautiful. Your skin is so soft. Your hair drives me crazy.* He traced every inch of her with his lips and fingers, and she repeated each move with hers. By the time he moved on top of her, spreading her legs wide, she was gasping for air, her entire body pulsing with need.

They made love twice before moving to the shower and making love a third time. Afterward he dried her hair and teased her body to the point of insanity all over again. He brought her to climax again with those magic fingers and those equally skilled lips, and then he held her tight until she drifted off to sleep.

Friday, October 21, 6:30 a.m.

SEAN WOKE TO the sweet scent of Amber. He smiled and resisted the urge to wake her. He wanted to make love to her again, but he had to be sure she wanted to go there. Last night had been an emotional one for her. He didn't want her to look back and see one minute of their time together as a mistake.

He was serious when he'd told her he wanted more than just one night together. If he was lucky, she would want the same. The idea of a serious relationship had been the furthest thought from his mind. Since Lacy, he hadn't wanted to feel this way again. Amber Roberts had shattered his defenses and stolen his ability to resist without even trying. He was pretty sure she had been as surprised by the development as he was.

Her eyes opened, and she stared at him in surprise. Holding his breath, he hoped regret wouldn't be the next emotion he saw in those beautiful green eyes. A smile widened across her kiss-swollen lips, and happiness was what he saw in her gaze.

"Good morning," she whispered.

He grinned. "It's a damned good morning." He brushed her lips with his own. "I was thinking we'd make pancakes. You like pancakes?"

She nibbled at his lips with her teeth. "I haven't indulged in pancakes in forever, but I'm not really ready to get out of bed yet." One delicate hand slid along his hip until those cool fingers found his arousal. "It feels like you're ready for something besides breakfast."

He teased a rosy nipple with his tongue. "Always."

They made love slowly. Her soft whimpers made him want to go faster, made him want to plunge hard and deep into her over and over, but he refused to hurry. He wanted to show her how important she was to him. How much he adored every part of her. How much he wanted to know her innermost thoughts and secrets.

His body arched with the building need as she cried out his name. He could hold back no longer. Still, he set an easy rhythm and pace, determined to make this last.

AFTER A SHOWER and a long morning walk, they were both ready for breakfast. She made the pancakes from a box of mix he found in the pantry. He brewed the coffee and rounded up the syrup.

"I don't know what your family does for the holidays," he ventured.

She licked her finger, making him smile. "Barb and Gina insist on hosting the family for Thanksgiving this year. We're eating lunch at one, so Barb and Gina can have the evening meal with the Colemans."

"That works out perfectly," he said, grabbing his courage with both hands. "Maybe you can come to dinner here with me and my family."

The smile started at one corner of her mouth and spread across her face, and the whole room lit up. "I could do that, if you're sure your family won't mind."

He downed a bite of pancake. "My family would be ecstatic. I warn you, though, they'll jump to conclusions. If you're not careful, my mother will start suggesting wedding venues."

Amber's tinkling laughter filled the air and made his heart glad. "I'm an expert at changing the subject."

He bit his tongue to prevent asking her if she had given up on the idea of weddings. He damned sure had—or he'd thought so. Funny, the notion of marriage didn't feel so difficult to imagine anymore. The realization should terrify him. Strangely it didn't.

Silence enveloped them for a minute or two. Sean recognized reality had intruded. They weren't kids punch-drunk after a night of incredible sex.

She set her fork aside. "What're we really doing, Sean?"

All of a sudden he didn't know how to answer that question. This—whatever it was—had happened so damned fast.

She nodded. "I can't answer the question, either." She exhaled a big breath. "I really like you. You make me feel things I haven't felt before, not even when I was wearing an engagement ring. I just don't know what it means."

"I'm in the same place." He shrugged. "I swore I'd never make this mistake again."

"Is that what *this* is? A mistake?"

The hurt in her eyes tightened his chest to the point where he couldn't draw in a decent breath. "I hope not." All that bravado he'd felt earlier abruptly deserted him. "I honestly don't know."

Obviously his answer wasn't the one she'd wanted to hear. "Wow. Okay." She stood and carried her plate to the sink.

Damn it. He grabbed his plate and joined her there. "I just meant—"

She backed away. "Let's not do this right now, okay?"

He piled his plate on top of hers and set his hands on his hips. "Is this your way of protecting your feelings? You just blow it off and walk away?" That was exactly what she was doing. Maybe instead of arguing he should take the easy way out and forget the whole damned thing.

"You're the one who called it a mistake."

Before he could respond, his cell in his pocket vibrated. He dug it out and glared at the screen. *The boss*. He dragged in a calming breath and answered. "Hey, boss. You have news?"

Sean listened to the update and tried to feel relief. Didn't happen. "Thanks. I'll let her know."

He ended the call and tucked his phone away. He had a bad feeling that what he was about to tell Amber would be the end of whatever *this* was. "The BPD found Thrasher. He's dead. He left a note apologizing for all he'd done."

Chapter Fifteen

"Peter Thrasher appears to have committed suicide. We can't officially call it a suicide until we have the autopsy report, but based on the ME's examination at the scene and the note he left, the preliminary call is suicide."

Lieutenant Chet Harper opened the folder in front of him and passed an eight-by-ten photo to Jess. Next to Sean, Amber tensed. He'd tried a dozen times on the way here to apologize for not being able to explain himself, but she refused to talk. She had been vulnerable, needy. He should have protected her without allowing personal feelings to get in the way. How could he make her see what he meant if she wouldn't hear him out?

He was supposed to be a professional. He

was supposed to keep her safe. He'd fallen down on both counts and he'd taken advantage of her need to grab on to life with both hands. He had to find a way to explain to her that the mistake he'd meant hadn't been what she thought.

Jess passed the photo to Sean, yanking him back to the present. The preliminary report indicated Thrasher appeared to have taken an overdose of over-the-counter sleep aids. The empty bottle had been found in his pocket. Apparently when he'd abandoned his car, he'd hitched a ride to the greenhouses where he grew flowers. One of his employees, a worker who spoke little or no English, had given him a ride. The employee had no idea Thrasher was embroiled in a murder investigation. He claimed Thrasher acted like he always did. When they had arrived at the greenhouses, Thrasher had told everyone to take the rest of the week off with pay.

"Forensics found evidence from both victims, McCorkle and Pettie, on Thrasher's computer. He and Adler were sharing the videos via a cloud service."

Jess studied the forensic report before passing it to Sean. "Is there any possibility the evidence was planted?"

Sean had been about to ask the same question. As badly as he'd screwed up with Amber, he hadn't forgotten the case entirely.

"Are you suggesting that someone may have set up Thrasher?" Amber asked. "The potential third killer you mentioned before?"

"That's exactly what I'm suggesting," Jess confirmed. "Thrasher knew the BPD was looking for him and he goes to a greenhouse and puts himself to permanent sleep? Why not just disappear? Did he call anyone on his cell? This is not typical behavior for a serial killer, and I'm always suspicious of an alleged suicide note that ties everything up in a nice, neat little bow."

Chet Harper shook his head. "We haven't located his cell. We're hoping to have his cell phone records later today." Harper directed his attention to Amber. "The case will remain open until we've tied up the last of the loose ends, but we're confident Adler and Thrasher murdered McCorkle and Pettie. It's difficult to say who actually did the killing or if it was a joint effort. As for the potential third perpetrator, we'll either rule out the scenario or we'll find him." When he turned back to Jess, he flared his hands. "Any additional input you have is always extremely valuable to the team."

"I agree with your conclusions to a degree." Jess surveyed the photos and reports now spread across the table. "But we're missing something."

"One other thing." Harper reached into another folder and removed a report. He passed it to Amber. "The toxin that made you sick was azalea leaves. Someone chopped up the leaves and added them to your tea. Do you have a regular tea routine?"

Amber looked from the report to Harper. "I have a cup every evening when I get home from work."

"Adler and Thrasher would have known that routine," Harper said. "Since Thrasher worked with flowers and small shrubs, we checked the greenhouses. He was growing a variety of azaleas. The lab is attempting to determine if the leaves in your tea came from a plant in his greenhouse. The azalea leaves may have been added to your tea to disable you. One or both men were likely watching, prepared to act when the time was right for abducting you."

Sean gritted his teeth. The son of a bitch's

carelessness with Amber's life made him want to beat the hell out of something…or someone.

"Did you find evidence that similar methods were used with McCorkle and Pettie?" Jess wanted to know.

"We've got the ME's office taking a second look," Harper confirmed. "Dr. Baron believes the screening tests wouldn't have picked up all potential plant toxins. She wants to run additional tests."

"I understand that the case is ongoing," Amber spoke up. "But are you saying Emma Norton and I are no longer in danger?"

Sean turned to Amber. She kept her gaze away from his. He'd made a mess of this morning and now she couldn't wait to get away from him. *Damn it.*

Harper and Jess exchanged a look. Harper said, "As far as the department is concerned, any threat these men posed no longer exists, but we are still investigating the possibility of a third person's involvement."

"I'm not completely comfortable with the facts in front of us," Jess said with obvious caution, "but to our knowledge the source of the threat is gone. If there is a third killer involved, he may believe he's tied up all the loose ends and will escape any consequences."

"But we can't be sure." The words were out of Sean's mouth before he'd taken the time to think through the statement.

All eyes were on him now. He might as well say the rest. "We can't say that Amber is no longer in danger until we rule out the third killer scenario."

A beat of silence echoed in the room.

"No doubt," Jess said, backing him up. "Amber." She turned her attention to the woman beside Sean. "The choice is yours. If you'd like to continue our security services a few days longer, we're more than happy to do so. Lieutenant Harper, I'm certain, will have more answers soon."

"I won't stop," Harper assured her, "until we know for certain. You have my word on that, Ms. Roberts."

Sean braced for Amber's decision.

"The cameras have been removed from my home," she said. "Adler and Thrasher are no longer a threat." She took a breath. "At this point, I feel secure on my own. I'll, of course, be watchful." She met the gaze of everyone at the table except Sean. "I appreciate all you and the BPD have done to bring a swift conclusion to this nightmare."

"Amber," Sean protested, "you should—"

"Get back to work." She stood. "I've had way more time off than I'm comfortable taking." She flashed a smile at Jess and Harper but still refused to even glance at Sean. "Thank you again."

"If you change your mind," Jess offered, "call. Day or night. We'll be there."

Amber gave her a nod and started for the door.

Sean pushed back from the conference table and followed her. He would owe his boss an explanation, but right now he couldn't let Amber leave this way.

"Amber, wait." He caught up with her at the elevator.

She jabbed the call button and reluctantly met his gaze. "We both have careers that need our attention, Sean. We don't need any distractions or personal entanglements. Spending more time together would complicate things. I'm not ready for complications. Clearly you aren't, either."

He touched her, wrapped his fingers around her forearm. Even that innocent contact made his pulse rush. "We should talk about us first."

For one instant he thought she was going to agree, but then her green eyes shuttered. "There is no us, Sean." She pulled free of his touch. "I have a very important event to attend tonight. Everybody who's anybody in Birmingham will be there—including your boss. I barely have time to pick up my dress from Martha's and get ready. Goodbye, Sean."

The elevator doors slid open, and she stepped inside. Sean watched her go. There was plenty he wanted to say, but none of it would come to him just now.

Eagle Ridge Drive, 2:00 p.m.

SEAN CLIMBED OUT of his car. Maybe he was way off base, but like his boss he wasn't convinced this case was as cut-and-dried as it seemed. It didn't feel right. He fully understood that part of what he felt was prompted by his feelings for Amber.

God almighty, he couldn't pretend those feelings didn't exist.

Problem was, he had his work cut out for him. Convincing Amber to give *them* a chance wasn't going to be easy. He had to find the right words to rebuild the trust he'd crushed with this morning's hurtful ones. Before he could worry about their relationship, he had to do whatever necessary to ensure she was safe.

He moved around to the back of Adler's

house. What he was about to do was breaking and entering. At least the house was no longer a crime scene. His boss wouldn't be happy when she found out, but if he found a connection to a third killer, she would likely let his methods slide. He removed the lock pick from his pocket, glanced around and set to the task. He'd learned how to pick a lock from Buddy Corlew, but he wasn't supposed to tell Jess.

The door opened easily. Inside the place still smelled like blood. He wasn't exactly clear on what he expected to find. Mostly he intended to look until he was satisfied there was nothing to find. He pulled on a pair of latex gloves and started with the living room.

He scanned the framed photos, the books, unopened mail. As he moved through the house he checked drawers, shelves, cabinets and closets. Nothing.

Before closing the door to Adler's bedroom closet, he hesitated. Might as well check the guy's pockets and shoes. One by one, Sean went through his jackets, his shirts and his trousers. Nothing in the pockets.

"Damn it."

There was only one thing to do. Check out Thrasher's place.

Unfortunately, it was still a crime scene.

Killough Circle, 3:30 p.m.

SEAN WAS INSIDE Thrasher's house without a glitch. As he did at Adler's place, he moved from room to room, checking every available space.

He'd almost called it a bust, when he backed up to check a framed photo next to the television. A younger Thrasher with a couple of buddies. It wasn't the sort of thing the cops would consider relevant; still it was worth a look.

"Well, hell." Sean picked up the photo and scrutinized at it. There were three guys. Thrasher was in the middle, Adler on the left. Sean studied the dark-haired guy on the right. The kid, seventeen or eighteen, looked vaguely familiar. He flipped the frame over and removed the back. As he'd hoped, the names were written on the back of the photo. Thrasher, Adler and Guynes. Where had he heard that name? The three looked high school age. The clothes were definitely last decade's.

Sean went back to the spare bedroom and opened the closet door. School yearbooks were piled on the top shelf. He grabbed the stack and went through the autographed pages. The threesome had been friends for years. Maybe they'd lost touch, but then why keep the framed photo displayed? People, especially men, didn't do that unless the people in the photograph were more than a little important to their lives.

The senior yearbook gave him the answer he was looking for. Delbert Guynes had been injured in a football game his senior year. Making the winning touchdown, he'd suffered a spinal cord injury, which had left him paralyzed from the waist down. Sean skimmed the dedication page. Guynes was touted as a hero, as was his mother who always tailored the cheerleader uniforms.

Martha Guynes... Martha Sews.

She had spoken as if she hardly knew Adler. She certainly hadn't mentioned that her son and Adler were best friends all through high school.

Amber was picking up a dress there today.

Sean shook his head. The theory didn't make sense. Delbert Guynes was paralyzed and sentenced to using a wheelchair for the rest of his life. He was a big video game player. Did that mean he was also a computer buff? What did a guy whose life consisted of being stuck in a wheelchair and under his mother's thumb do for fun...or for pleasure? *The videos*. Maybe the cameras had been for Delbert.

Still, how could Delbert be involved with Adler and Thrasher's criminal activities without his mother knowing?

Memories from his and Amber's visit to the shop the other day flashed one after the other through Sean's mind.

Were those shrubs lining the front of her shop azaleas?

Martha Sews, 4:30 p.m.

AMBER PEERED OVER her shoulder at the mirror. The back of the dress looked great. She smiled. "It's perfect, Martha." She turned back to the lady who had single-handedly kept Amber's wardrobe fitting right for years now. Being what the fashion world considered petite was a real pain. Not even the most expensive labels managed to make clothes that fit her body. "I don't know what I'd do without you."

Martha beamed. "I love taking care of you, Amber. You're my favorite customer."

Amber gave her another big smile before stepping back into the dressing room. "I'll change and pay so you can call it a day." It had to be five already. Thankfully that still left her enough time to get ready.

"Take your time. I'm locking up," Martha

called. "Would you like some tea before you fight the rush hour traffic?"

Arching her back, Amber reached for the zipper. "Oh, that would be wonderful."

"Paradise Peach still your favorite?"

Amber almost stumbled stepping out of the dress. "Yes." She cleared her throat. "But whatever you have will be fine." Her stomach roiled. The ugly few hours she'd endured the other night had made her wonder if she would ever drink another cup of her favorite tea. Her response to Martha had been automatic. Amber's grandmother had taught her to love hot tea. Louisa Roberts would be immensely offended that someone would use tea as a weapon.

"I have tea cakes if you'd like one," Martha called. "You should treat yourself more often, Amber. You deserve it."

Amber paused again as she wiggled into the unwashed jeans she'd bought yesterday. She tugged the sweater on next. The memory of rushing through the discount store grabbing clothes with Sean made her heart hurt. How had he stolen a place in her heart in a mere four days? She hadn't meant to let that happen, but control had been taken from her so quickly her head was still spinning. Walking out of that meeting on her own today had been her way of taking back control. Adler and Thrasher were dead. She would be okay.

"You'll love the cakes," Martha said loud enough for Amber to hear. "They're my grandmother's recipe."

Evicting thoughts of Sean, Amber considered that she really wouldn't have time to eat before heading to the fund-raiser. A quick snack would be nice. "I would love a tea cake."

She stepped out of the dressing room, and Martha was waiting for her. Amber jumped.

"I'm sorry. I didn't mean to startle you, dear." She took the dress from Amber's hand. "Come along before your tea gets cold."

"You don't want me to pay you first?" Amber followed her to the kitchen.

"That won't be necessary." Martha draped the dress across the back of a chair. "Sit down and I'll serve."

Amber exhaled, feeling a burst of uncertainty. What was wrong with her? This was Martha. She'd known her for years. There was time before she had to get dressed. She needed to relax. If she were honest with herself, she would admit that it was Sean. Making love with him had touched her in a place no one had reached before. It was ridiculous. She barely knew the man and somehow it felt as if they'd always known each other. He felt like the perfect fit…her other half.

Ridiculous. Tomorrow Sean would wake up and realize the circumstances had triggered an out-of-control moment, and he'd never think of her again.

"Amber?"

She snapped to attention. "I'm sorry—what did you say?"

"I was asking about your friend Mr. Douglas."

"Oh." Amber accepted the cup of tea. "His assignment concluded."

"So you were working together." Martha gestured to a chair. She then placed a tea cake on a delicate china plate and set it in front of Amber.

"We were." *Close enough*, she supposed as she sipped the warm refreshment.

"He seemed like a nice young man." Martha settled into a chair across the table from Amber. "Quite handsome. I thought he was smitten with you—the way he looked at you, I mean."

"I…don't think so." Amber sipped her tea to avoid saying more.

"You certainly appeared quite taken with him."

Before Amber could protest, a howl reverberated through the house.

Martha jumped up from her seat. "Delbert?" She rushed from the room.

Amber sat there for a moment, wondering if she should check to see if everything was all right. The silence that followed felt entirely wrong. She should see if Martha and her son were okay.

Amber stood and the room tilted.

Good grief. What was wrong with her?

She stared at the porcelain cup. *The tea.*

Where was her phone? Her purse?

Turning around, Amber grabbed at that table to maintain her balance.

"Now, now, take care there."

Amber tried to steady herself. Martha was suddenly at her side, guiding her forward. At least it felt as if they were moving.

"Martha…" Amber's tongue wouldn't work right. She felt horribly ill. Vomiting felt imminent.

"Don't you worry, dear. I'm going to take extra good care of you."

Amber leaned heavily on Martha. She couldn't hold herself up anymore. She tried to plead with her…but the words wouldn't come out.

"Here she is, Delbert."

Amber felt her body plop into a chair. The room was shifting again. In front of her a man in a wheelchair stared at her. Delbert. Martha's son. Behind him the computer screen that usually sported a video game was focused on a small room. Was that the dressing room she'd just been using to try on the dress? Amber groaned. She couldn't be sure. Her vision kept fading in and out. She just didn't know. She felt horribly sick.

"We thought we'd lost you," Martha was saying.

What was she talking about?

"You're the one he wanted," Martha cooed. "Of all the ones we offered, it was you he wanted."

Amber didn't understand. She tried to move. Couldn't.

"Rhiana turned out to be nothing but a whore." Martha heaved a big sign as she knelt in front of Amber and tied her feet together.

Amber told herself to pull away from her. To get up and run, but her legs wouldn't work.

"And Kimberly was a closet alcoholic. He just didn't like either of the two the boys and I picked out for him. It was you. It had always been you. He'd been watching you for years. He said you were perfect. You were the one. I even tried to discourage him. How could someone as famous as you be bothered, but then I understood what I had to do. I had to make you available."

Amber tried again to cry out. She tried to get up. Her body wouldn't work.

"And those stupid so-called friends of his almost ruined everything. You just can't depend on anyone anymore. They were only supposed to install the cameras on the candidates. But I knew when Kimberly went missing that they were up to something. The bastards were messing with those girls, and they killed them. But don't worry—I took care of those idiots. As soon as I found out what they were up to, I made them pay. All I had to do after that was find a way to get you here. I'm sorry about the tea the other night. That wasn't supposed to happen until I was ready. You'll be fine, though. I was careful about the dosage."

She tied Amber's wrists together. "Now. We're ready. I'm going to be taking you and Delbert to a special place where no one will ever bother us. You are to love him and take care of him from now on. He's ready for a life of his own, and he has chosen you to share it with him. I'll make sure you have whatever you need."

Another of those eerie howls echoed in the room.

"Hush now, Delbert. She's all yours." Martha got to her feet. "You can play with her all you want, every day from now on, and she'll take good care of you."

Amber closed her eyes in an effort to stop the spinning. She had to do something.

Martha screamed, and Amber's eyes snapped open.

Sean.

Her heart leaped. He was here.

He and Martha struggled. Amber tried to keep her eyes open, but she couldn't.

The darkness consumed her...and then the silence.

UAB Hospital

AMBER OPENED HER EYES. She felt weak. Her brain seemed swaddled with cotton. She remembered throwing up in the ambulance. She remembered... *Sean.* He'd been right beside her through it all.

"There you are." His blue eyes twinkled as he smiled at her.

Her heart squeezed. She really liked his smile. She like his eyes and everything else about him. "Martha…oh, my God." Her mouth felt cotton dry. "She's done my alterations for years. How did you know?"

"Thrasher kept a framed photo of him and his best buds from high school—Kyle Adler and Delbert Guynes. I couldn't get the idea out of my head that there was a third player in all this. When I saw that photo, I knew I was right."

Amber reached for the water on the bedside table. "Let me do that." Sean poured water in the cup and added a bendable straw; then he held it to her lips. "This should help."

The water cooled her raw throat. She drew back and he set the cup aside. "I don't see how Martha thought she could get away with this." Amber shook her head. "They were helping her find a caregiver for Delbert. Why in the world would she do something so insane? She always seemed so normal." The whole idea was ludicrous.

"Jess called a little while ago and gave me an update." Sean's expression turned somber. "Martha is dying. It's cancer. The doctors have given her maybe six months to live. She doesn't want her son in some institution. When she found out Thrasher and Adler were using her shop to video women changing and then sharing that video with her son, she threatened to call the police."

"Wait." Amber's brain was still a little fuzzy from the poisoned tea. "Why did she threaten to call the police?"

"To make them cooperate with her. At some point after that she found out they were using the women for sex slaves. She killed Adler when she found out he was obsessed with you. She was after Thrasher next, so he killed himself. He knew his life was over anyway, so he ended it himself. Martha found him and left the note."

"The whole thing is just horrible." Amber fiddled with the edge of the stiff sheet. "What happens to Delbert now?"

Sean took her hands in his. "He'll be placed in a facility and receive the care he needs. It isn't what his mother wanted, but there's no other family. The important thing is that you're safe now and the Pettie and McCorkle families don't have to wonder if their daughters' killers will get away with murder."

"You were right." Amber squeezed his hand, tears burning in her eyes. "Still waters do run deep."

"Sometimes being right is not so much fun." He leaned forward and kissed her forehead.

"I was thinking," she ventured. "I feel like maybe it's time we learned how to have a real personal life. Together, I mean. Unless, of course, you really believe what happened was a mistake."

"You're behind the curve, Roberts." He grinned and shot her a wink. "I've already started. For the record, I never thought what happened between us was a mistake. I worried that the circumstances were the wrong time and place." He kissed her hands. "I don't care what brought me to you, all that matters is that I found you. I want to explore what we have more than I want to see the sun come up tomorrow."

That was the best news she'd heard all week. "I'm sure we can arrange for both to happen."

"Good." He kissed her lips this time.

Amber closed her eyes and savored the sound of his deep voice as he promised her the world. As soon as she was out of this hospital she intended to hold him to every single one of those promises.

Chapter Sixteen

3309 Dell Road, Mountain Brook, 9:00 p.m.

"She's growing too fast." Jess smoothed the hair back from her sweet baby girl's face.

Dan tucked the pink blanket around Bea. He turned to Jess, took her by the hands and drew her away from their daughter's crib. "She'll always be our little girl no matter how big she gets."

Jess leaned into his chest and closed her eyes as his arms went around her. "Is she going to be jealous of her little brother?" Jess peered up at him. "I don't think I could bear it if they hate each other when they become teenagers. Lil and I went through that stage, you know."

"You need some hot cocoa." Dan kissed her forehead and ushered her from Bea's room.

He looked back one last time before turning out the light. The princess night-light kept the room from being completely dark. Jess had always been afraid of the dark. She hoped her children weren't, but just in case she intended to make sure they felt safe.

"We have to finish decorating your son's room soon. He'll be here before we know it." She was feeling a little overwhelmed lately. The agency was off to a great start and even Sean had turned out to be a top-notch member of the team. Still, there was just so much to do, and she felt tired all the time.

Dan guided her to her favorite chair in their family room. Toys were scattered all over the floor. Jess groaned. She had sworn she would never be one of those people—the ones who spoil their children with far too many toys. And look at their home. Toys were lying about in every room.

"You sit tight, and I'll make the hot chocolate." He backed toward the door and stumbled when the stuffed animal he stepped on made a high-pitched sound. He swore under his breath and snatched up the pink bear to ensure it still worked. It did not.

"You killed it," Jess warned. "You better get rid of it before she notices."

Dan nodded. "Good idea."

He hurried away, damaged pink bear in hand.

Jess huffed out a big breath. This was her mother-in-law's fault. Katherine spoiled Bea endlessly. "Like you don't," she muttered.

With much effort and no shortage of groaning, Jess hefted herself out of the big plush chair and followed the path Dan had taken to the kitchen. He'd just put the milk in the microwave. She slid onto a stool at the island and watched as he readied the instant cocoa mix. It might be instant, but it tasted like the real thing. With a toddler in the house, they had both learned to appreciate plenty of *instant* fixes.

"What's on your mind?" Her handsome husband leaned on the island and studied her. "I can always tell when you're unsettled."

It was true. They had been in love since they were teenagers and could read each other like a book.

"This case reminded me of the one that brought me back home." The similarities were disturbing.

Dan nodded. "Me, too. I was terrified Andrea would end up dead, like the two women in this case."

Jess placed her hand on his arm and smiled. "But she didn't. She's in her senior year of college and doing great." Andrea was Dan's stepdaughter from a previous marriage. Though the marriage had been over for years, Dan still loved Andrea. Jess did, as well. She was a wonderful young woman.

"She didn't because you found her when no one else could." He touched Jess's cheek. "I am so thankful you came back to me."

"This is where I was always supposed to be."

The microwave dinged and he straightened away from the island. "First you had to go catch all those serial killers for the FBI."

She rubbed her belly as Dan prepared her cocoa. One of those bad guys had followed her back to Birmingham and no matter that two years had passed since she ended his reign of terror, he still haunted her sometimes.

The steaming cocoa appeared in front of her, marshmallows floating on top. "Drink up before it gets cold."

She arranged her lips into a smile. "Thank you. Where's yours?"

"I—" he reached into the fridge "—am having a beer."

She made a face. "Don't brag."

He twisted the top off the glass bottle. "The case brought up memories of Spears and

Holmes." He traced his fingers over her forehead. "Whenever you're worried about a case you frown. And since the big case B&C was investigating is closed, it has to be about those two bastards."

He knew her too well. "Spears is dead. I don't worry about him. It's all his sick followers that keep me awake sometimes." Ted Holmes had tried his best to reenact Spears's obsession with her. He'd gotten far too close to her child. "I've had my moments since leaving the department," she confessed, "when I thought I'd made a mistake. That maybe I couldn't do as much to stop the evil out there."

Dan held his tongue and allowed her to continue in her own time.

"This case showed me I made the right decision." She held up her mug. "To the future."

Dan tapped her mug with his bottle of beer. "Hear, hear."

One more face of evil down. Jess sipped her hot cocoa and relished the victory.

* * * * *

Look for more FACES OF EVIL
coming in 2017 only from
Debra Webb and Harlequin Intrigue!

But first, read a sneak peek of
THE BLACKEST CRIMSON,
the prequel for the upcoming
SHADES OF DEATH *series.*

Don't miss this thrilling new series from
MIRA *books and Debra Webb*
coming in March 2017!

Chapter One

Brisbane Place, Montgomery, Alabama
Friday, December 24, 6:30 p.m.

"It's snowing!" Detective Bobbie Gentry smiled, her heart feeling glad for the first time in nearly a month. It rarely snowed for Christmas in Alabama. If they were lucky enough to get snow, it usually showed up in January or February. She pressed her hand to the glass of the big bay window that overlooked their front yard. All the houses in the cul-de-sac, including theirs, were decorated with twinkling lights and garland, chasing away the darkness of the cold winter night. She needed this Christmas to be peaceful. She yearned for the normalcy of family, for the roar and crackle of a fire as they gathered around the tree they had spent the day decorating.

A contented sigh slipped past her lips. The

way those big flakes were falling the neighborhood would look like a classic holiday greeting card within the hour. Maybe tonight would make up for the endless hours of overtime and weekends away from her family she'd put in this month.

Her husband moved up behind her and circled her waist with his arms. "Man, it's really coming down out there. The weatherman said we're on the lower edge of the storm, but we could get several inches. Maybe more. Wouldn't that be nice?"

"Very nice." Bobbie leaned into him and covered his forearms with hers. A snowstorm bringing more than an inch or two was nearly unheard of this far south. Suited her just fine. In fact, the timing couldn't be better. Today was her first day off this month. She'd slept late, and she'd been wearing her husband's Alabama sweatshirt and her lounge pants all day. She might not bother with real clothes until after the holidays. She was so damned glad just to be home. "I really needed this."

James nuzzled her neck. "I'm glad it's over."

Would it ever really be over? The killer was still out there. God only knew where.

For the last three weeks Bobbie and her partner had been working with the FBI on a serial murder case. The Storyteller. If she lived ten lifetimes, she wouldn't be able to adequately clear the horrors she had seen and heard from her mind. The images of his victims…the endless reports and profiles about the unknown subject's—the killer's—methodology and psychopathy. The Storyteller was the sickest bastard Bobbie had encountered during her career with law enforcement. If she was lucky, she would never encounter that level of pure evil again.

As rough as the past twenty or so days had been, she was home tonight. She could stand right here for hours and watch the beauty of nature turn the landscape white. Her mother had once told her that snow was a gift from God to brighten the long dark winters. Those words had never been truer than they were at this moment.

Bobbie turned in her husband's arms and smiled. "Thank you for taking care of everything while…" She shook her head. "While I was so tied up. I was afraid our son wouldn't even remember who I was."

James pressed his forehead to hers. "No need to thank me." His arms tightened around her waist. "And, for your information, our son thinks you're a superhero."

She searched his eyes, so very grateful for this wonderful man. "Really?"

James nodded. "I told him Mommy was keeping the monsters away."

"Mommy!"

Jamie slammed into Bobbie's legs. She leaned down and scooped up her little boy. "Look at all the snow. Tomorrow we can make a snowman with Daddy."

"Santa help, too?"

Bobbie kissed his soft cheek, inhaled his baby-shampoo scent. He was growing up so fast. In just four months he would be three years old. She wished time would slow down just a little. "I don't know about Santa, sweetie. Tomorrow's Christmas, and he'll be very busy."

Her precious little boy had blond hair and gray eyes exactly like his father. Jamie had made her life complete. As much as she valued her career as a homicide detective, this—she smiled at her husband and then at their child—was her world. Maybe one of these days Jamie would have a little brother or sister. She and James had discussed the possibility after making love that morning. Bobbie was ready.

Jamie pressed his forehead against her cheek. "Wudolph."

She grinned. "Is it time for Rudolph?"

Her son nodded, those big gray eyes twinkling with anticipation.

"Start the movie." James ushered them toward the sofa. "I'll put the cookies for Santa in the oven."

"Santa! Santa!" Jamie bounced in Bobbie's arms.

"Thanks." She gave her handsome husband a kiss on the jaw.

He smiled. "Love you."

"Love you more."

"Wuv you!" Jamie shouted in his sweet little boy voice.

"Wuv you, buddy." James backed toward the kitchen. "Save me a seat."

"You got it," Bobbie promised.

Curling up on the sofa, Jamie snuggled in next to her. She picked up the remote, found the movie they had recorded on the DVR and saved just for tonight, and then hit Play. As the credits rolled and the celebrated Christmas song began to play, Bobbie sang along. "Rudolph, the red-nosed reindeer…"

Jamie burst into his own rendition of the tune, and her heart swelled with happiness. She kissed the top of his blond head and hugged him tight.

A crash in the kitchen had her twisting

around toward the entry hall that led from the front door, past the living room and dining room and into the kitchen. Their home was a traditional center hall Southern colonial, and she loved it. It wasn't the popular open concept, but the entire downstairs flowed from one room to the next.

"You having trouble with those cookies, James?" she teased.

Burl Ives's deep baritone filled the room. Jamie was mesmerized by the classic animation. But it was the silence in the kitchen that held Bobbie in an ever-tightening grip. The fine hair on the back of her neck stood on end while her pulse bumped into a faster rhythm. She eased away from Jamie and moved around the sofa. "James?"

A clang echoed from the kitchen.

For an endless moment time seemed to stop, even as denial and a hundred explanations that didn't include what she understood was happening whirled in her head. Her gaze settled on the stairs. Her service revolver was in the lockbox on her bedside table. Seventeen steps up and then ten yards to the end of the hall; the door was on the left.

No time to go for it.

Adrenaline fired in her blood, jolting her

into action. Bobbie reached across the back of the sofa and grabbed Jamie. Ignoring his protests, she ran to the front door. As she twisted the lock, her heart slamming mercilessly against her sternum, she heard the *clump-clump-clump* of rushing footfalls behind her.

Hurry!

She jerked the door open and thrust her child onto the porch.

"Run, Jamie!" she screamed, frantic determination and utter certainty of what was coming coalescing into sheer terror.

Her little boy stared up at her, scared and confused, with those precious, precious gray eyes.

"Run for help like Mommy showed you!"

Brutal fingers fisted in her hair and jerked her back. She kicked at the door, sending it slamming closed. She prayed her baby would run to the neighbor's house for help the way she had taught him. Over and over they had practiced what he was to do if she ever told him to run because something bad happened.

Please, please, please, keep him safe.

"Merry Christmas, Detective Gentry," a deep voice announced.

A sweater-clad forearm looped around her throat and dragged her backward. Her gaze zoomed in on the bloody knife in the hand at the end of that arm.

"James!"

The sound of her husband's name echoing around her snapped her from the strange frozen place she'd slipped into. She clawed at the arm. Twisted to get free.

"I should be halfway across Mississippi by now," the voice—male—said with a snarl. "But I simply couldn't leave without coming back for you. I've done nothing but fantasize about you for weeks."

Bobbie tried to dig her heels into the floor to slow down his momentum, but he was too strong. She gasped for air as his arm tightened on her throat.

Think, Bobbie!

Relax. Let him believe he's won. She stopped struggling. Just let him drag her limp body as if she'd lost consciousness. The hardwood turned to tile. He was taking her into the kitchen. James was in the kitchen. *Please, please, please, let him be okay.*

The bastard jerked her upright, yanking her around to face him and pinned her against the island with his body. The bloody blade of the knife pressed against her throat. "I've never had a detective before. I can't wait to write your story, Bobbie."

Oh, dear God. This couldn't be happening. The Storyteller never struck twice in the same place. No one knew his name…or had seen his face.

"You are so beautiful," he whispered roughly. "Even more beautiful than Alyssa or any of the others."

Bobbie bit back the rage she wanted to hurl at him. Alyssa Powell had been his last victim. The one he'd brought from Georgia and dumped in the Montgomery PD's jurisdiction.

"We're going to have so much fun together."

Look at him, Bobbie! Commit his features to memory. Brown hair and eyes. Soft jaw, narrow nose. Five-ten or five-eleven. One seventy or eighty pounds. Late thirties. No noticeable facial scars or moles.

"We should go," the bastard said. "That kid of yours has probably alerted the neighbors, who will no doubt call the police. They'll surround your lovely home and make our escape problematic. Can't have that."

This was it. He was taking her.

Wait…where was James? Her heart threatened to burst. *Please, please, don't let him be dead.*

"Be a good girl now."

The blade moved a fraction of an inch from her throat, and she snapped into action, ramming her knee upward. He pivoted. She nailed his hip instead of his groin. *Damn it!* She clawed at his eyes. The blade slid across her forearm, slicing deep. She screamed and punched him in the face with all her might.

He grabbed a handful of her hair before she could twist away and slammed her head against the island's unforgiving granite countertop. Pain split her skull. Her muscles went lax. The warmth of urine spread down her thighs.

She was falling…falling. Her body crumpled to the tile. She blinked, her vision narrowing.

Suddenly she was moving again. He was dragging her by her arm…moving toward the side exit to the garage.

Leaving.

James… Where was James?

Her lids drooped lower, almost closing, but not before she saw her husband on the floor… his beautiful gray eyes wide-open, frozen in fear…mouth slack.

The tile around him was no longer white… it was the blackest crimson.

LARGER-PRINT BOOKS!

LARGER-PRINT BOOKS!

GET 2 FREE LARGER-PRINT NOVELS PLUS
2 FREE GIFTS!

♦HARLEQUIN®

Romance

From the Heart, For the Heart

LARGER-PRINT BOOKS!
GET 2 FREE LARGER-PRINT NOVELS PLUS
2 FREE GIFTS!

HARLEQUIN®

super romance®

More Story...More Romance

YES! Please send me 2 FREE LARGER-PRINT Harlequin® Superromance® novels and my 2 FREE gifts (gifts are worth about $10). After receiving them, if I don't wish to receive any more books, I can return the shipping statement marked "cancel." If I don't cancel, I will receive 4 brand-new novels every month and be billed just $5.94 per book in the U.S. or $6.24 per book in Canada. That's a savings of at least 12% off the cover price! It's quite a bargain! Shipping and handling is just 50¢ per book in the U.S. or 75¢ per book in Canada.* I understand that accepting the 2 free books and gifts places me under no obligation to buy anything. I can always return a shipment and cancel at any time. Even if I never buy another book, the two free books and gifts are mine to keep forever.

132/332 HDN GHVC

Name	(PLEASE PRINT)	
Address		Apt. #
City	State/Prov.	Zip/Postal Code

Signature (if under 18, a parent or guardian must sign)

Mail to the **Reader Service:**
IN U.S.A.: P.O. Box 1867, Buffalo, NY 14240-1867
IN CANADA: P.O. Box 609, Fort Erie, Ontario L2A 5X3

Want to try two free books from another line?
Call 1-800-873-8635 today or visit www.ReaderService.com.

* Terms and prices subject to change without notice. Prices do not include applicable taxes. Sales tax applicable in N.Y. Canadian residents will be charged applicable taxes. Offer not valid in Quebec. This offer is limited to one order per household. Not valid for current subscribers to Harlequin Superromance Larger-Print books. All orders subject to credit approval. Credit or debit balances in a customer's account(s) may be offset by any other outstanding balance owed by or to the customer. Please allow 4 to 6 weeks for delivery. Offer available while quantities last.

Your Privacy—The Reader Service is committed to protecting your privacy. Our Privacy Policy is available online at www.ReaderService.com or upon request from the Reader Service.

We make a portion of our mailing list available to reputable third parties that offer products we believe may interest you. If you prefer that we not exchange your name with third parties, or if you wish to clarify or modify your communication preferences, please visit us at www.ReaderService.com/consumerschoice or write to us at Reader Service Preference Service, P.O. Box 9062, Buffalo, NY 14240-9062. Include your complete name and address.

HSRLP15

WESTERN WP PROMISES

YES! Please send me **The Western Promises Collection** in Larger Print. This collection begins with 3 FREE books and 2 FREE gifts (gifts valued at approx. $14.00 retail) in the first shipment, along with the other first 4 books from the collection! If I do not cancel, I will receive 8 monthly shipments until I have the entire 51-book Western Promises collection. I will receive 2 or 3 FREE books in each shipment and I will pay just $4.99 US/ $5.89 CDN for each of the other four books in each shipment, plus $2.99 for shipping and handling per shipment. *If I decide to keep the entire collection, I'll have paid for only 32 books, because 19 books are FREE! I understand that accepting the 3 free books and gifts places me under no obligation to buy anything. I can always return a shipment and cancel at any time. My free books and gifts are mine to keep no matter what I decide.

272 HCN 3070 472 HCN 3070

Name	(PLEASE PRINT)	
Address		Apt. #
City	State/Prov.	Zip/Postal Code

Signature (if under 18, a parent or guardian must sign)

Mail to the **Reader Service:**

IN U.S.A.: P.O. Box 1867, Buffalo, NY 14240-1867
IN CANADA: P.O. Box 609, Fort Erie, Ontario L2A 5X3

* Terms and prices subject to change without notice. Prices do not include applicable taxes. Sales tax applicable in N.Y. Canadian residents will be charged applicable taxes. This offer is limited to one order per household. All orders subject to approval. Credit or debit balances in a customer's account(s) may be offset by any other outstanding balance owed by or to the customer. Please allow 4 to 6 weeks for delivery. Offer available while quantities last. Offer not available to Quebec residents.

WPBPA16R